Coffee, Bagels and Murder
C. FARREN

Coffee, Angels, and Murder

The Snowflake Bay Cozy Mysteries, Volume 1

C. Farren

Published by David Dawson, 2020.

This is a work of fiction. Similarities to real people, places, or events are entirely coincidental.

COFFEE, ANGELS, AND MURDER

First edition. December 2, 2020.

Copyright © 2020 C. Farren.

Written by C. Farren.

Table of Contents

Dedicated to John Fisher and Valerie King

6

Chapter 1

"Am I boring you?" Cedric asked.

Wren regarded the man sitting opposite her, snapping out of her daydream. The two of them were in a cheap Italian restaurant that had the ambiance of a morgue. She wore a sexy black dress that had failed to even solicit a single compliment from her date and her new hairdo cost more than her shoes. He was wearing a jolly red sweater that stank of mildew and his hair was combed over. He kept putting his hand on his stomach, as if forgetting it was even there. There was a handsome man in there somewhere, she was sure.

Outside it was raining heavily, threatening to give the streets a shiny glow.

"Yes, of course," Wren answered. She struggled to recall what they'd been talking about. "The weather is quite chilly, no?"

Cedric sighed. "I was telling you all about the new sealant gel we were using in our windows."

"How could I forget?" Wren quipped. Keeping the sarcasm out of her voice was almost torture. "Such a fascinating subject."

He started going on again, and Wren tuned him out. *Why had I even agreed to go out with him?* She sighed sadly, realizing why. Cedric Roper was attractive, in a sort of Bob Hoskins meets George Clooney kind of way, but he was about as interesting as reading the back of a Corn Flakes box. Still, it was an evening out and, as her gran used to say, never turn down a free meal.

"I used to be married you know," he explained. Wren perked up a little. This was information she didn't know. "She didn't like me talking about the business either. No wonder she left me."

"I'm sorry," she said.

He bit his lip, as if holding back something. "It's been twenty years. I've gotten over it. Yes." He looked down at his dinner sadly before adding, "I've gotten over it."

Wren smiled politely. She was starting to feel uncomfortable now. Cedric was older than he appeared. He looked to be in his late thirties, but if he'd been married twenty years ago, he must have been, a lot older than she'd imagined.

"Where do you see yourself in five years, Wren?" Cedric asked.

The question startled her. She'd never thought about it before. A job? Marriage? Kids? A 4K television in the bathroom? *I so want to get out of here, but it looks cold outside, and I'd probably freeze to death in this dress.*

"I honestly don't know," she admitted. The thought made her feel inadequate and somehow, lost. "I'd like to think I'd be in a better place than I am now."

He nodded. "So, you've never considered marriage?".

Cedric was scoping her out for the future. He was actually seriously interested in her, and she was so bored to tears she imagined that watching paint dry was more exciting.

"I was married once too," Wren admitted. She stared down at the remnants of the slightly burnt cheese sauce on her plate. The restaurant's owner, Lala di Campo, was staring daggers at her from behind the bar. "But it was a long time ago."

"It didn't go well?" he asked.

She didn't like to dwell on the past. "I'm surprised you don't know. It was the talk of the town."

"I don't listen to idle gossip."

She had to end this now before things got any further. She didn't want to hurt this man's feelings, but she had no choice. She had to be brutally honest.

"This is not going great," Wren admitted. She looked him in the eye. He didn't blink. "I think I'm going to just go home."

"Do your cats need feeding?" he asked sulkily.

"I don't have any cats!" she shouted.

Wren stormed off, almost tripping over the carpet in her haste to escape. She started to cry. The truth was, she did have a cat and she loved the silly little fur ball more than anything else in her barren life. A 35-year-old woman with a cat screamed out "old spinster" and she'd wanted to leave the table with a little of her dignity intact.

Even though I do have cheese sauce on my dress.

When Wren got outside, she realized, as fat droplets of rain battered her bare arms, that she'd left her coat inside the restaurant.

She slipped quietly back inside, grabbed her coat, and ran back out as fast as her legs could carry her.

WREN STOOD ON THE EDGE of the docks, hugging herself to keep warm. The sea was calm, pretty even, as the rain turned into a light drizzle around her. She felt peaceful and calm and not quite ready to head home just yet. Going home meant accepting defeat and admitting that her love life truly was an epic disaster.

The marina was silent, most of the boats at the dock unused for years, ever since the fish stocks dried up. The fishermen had moved away soon after and the town's economy had almost collapsed. The only good thing they had going for them was the Hollywood movie that had been filmed there twenty years ago. Tourists flocked here in the summer to see the place that a hunky merman rescued a drowned Nicole Kidman.

Wren laughed. Truth be told, she hated *Love by the Sea*. It was sappy and depressing and the tourists were a pain in the neck. She should know, she'd worked in the tourist center for eight years before things turned sour with her boss.

Don't think about him. It'll only upset you.

The wooden decking creaked behind her. Wren tensed, ready to defend herself. After being mugged once many years ago, she'd learned a little taekwondo at a women's self-defense class. She still sometimes attended classes with her mother when she was bored. No one would get the upper hand on her ever again.

"Stay back," she screamed, tense. Her hands were weapons! "I have a mace in my bag and I'm not afraid to use it!"

The intruder was a tall man, wrapped up in a thick blue winter coat. The hood half covered his head, and the only thing she could make out in the dark and the light rain were a mesmerizing set of twinkling brown eyes.

"Sorry," he said. His voice was deep, with a slight British accent. "I just needed a bit of fresh air. I didn't mean to startle you."

Wren crossed her arms. She didn't sense any hostility from the man. His eyes conveyed to her simple curiosity and warm humor, nothing more. But what was he doing on the docks all on his own this late at night anyway?

"You mean you've got mace, right?" he asked.

"I beg your pardon?" she asked, confused.

"You said you had a mace in your bag," he said. "I presume you didn't mean the medieval weapon that could cave in a bear's skull?"

Wren grinned. "No, and I don't have any mace either. My hands are my lethal weapons."

God, I sound so corny!

"What are you doing out here so late?" Wren asked.

"I was just scoping out the area," he said. "I'm thinking about buying a house in town. Is this a nice place to live?"

"It's fine if you like boring."

He held his gloved hand out. "I'm..."

The ringing of a cell phone interrupted his introduction. Wren wanted to scream in frustration but answered it. It was her mother, and it had to be urgent if she needed to interrupt her daughter on a date.

She was the one who nagged me into going on this date in the first place when I had misgivings about it. That woman really wants grandchildren. Or ready-made organ donors.

"Hello?" Wren screamed, turning away from the man so he couldn't see her face scrunched up in annoyance. "What is it?"

"Gracie's being sick all over the place and I tried to pick her up but she bit me and now she's on the fridge and I think she might be dying!" her mother blurted out.

Wren sighed. Her mother had insisted on cat sitting, despite her misgivings. Felines and sixty-year-old housewives with cat allergies and a low tolerance for mischief didn't mix.

"What did you feed her?" Wren asked.

"I was chopping up some onions to fry and I dropped one on the kitchen floor," her mother explained. "I made a grab for it but Gracie just bit into the thing and started chomping down on it."

"Onions are poisonous to cats! Oh God, Mom..."

She told her mother she'd be back as quickly as she could and hung up. The man in the winter coat was gone.

"Oh," she said, feeling disappointed.

It was the best conversation she'd had all year.

WREN PICKED UP HER precious cargo and gave her a kiss on the head. Gracie snuggled up to her chin, affectionate as always. The cat didn't seem in the least bit distressed, unlike her mother. She looked like she'd just survived the sinking of the Titanic.

"How is she?" Wren asked.

Her mother, Dorothy 'Dot' King, crossed her arms. "Evil incarnate is what she is."

"I am never going on a date ever again."

"Was it that bad?"

She played back Cedric's monotonous voice in her head and shuddered. She'd had a lucky escape there.

THE CAT MEOWED HER question again. Wren was too busy staring into a bowl of chocolate ice cream and enjoying the awful trashiness of her favorite soap, *Sunset Cove*. Was this what her life had become, eating garbage (albeit tasty, delicious garbage), and living her life through soaps?

She concentrated on the TV, pushing Cedric out of her mind. The hunky, bare chested hero, Favio, gripped his lover passionately. He looked deep into her eyes and said, "I'm going to take you to bed and make love to you all night long...no, all weekend. I won't stop until we're either dead or paralyzed!"

Sera tried to pull away, but you could tell she wasn't trying too hard. Favio was the hunk of hunks. Any woman would be lucky enough to have him.

"But what about my husband, your identical cousin?" Sera cried.

"He won't trouble us ever again."

Favio leaned in for a kiss, just as the action switched to Jedd, Favio's identical twin cousin. He was currently tied up on the deck of a sinking yacht, circled by sharks. He screamed for help just as the credits started to roll.

Wren stared down at Gracie and said, "No, my date went entirely as expected, as in really badly."

Gracie meowed again.

She smiled and patted her on the head. "What do you want me to say? It was worse than the date I went on with Keegan, and he came out of the closet half-way through."

They were both sixteen when they decided to go on a date. They both had the same birthday, and had been friends since kindergarten, and had thought it might be fun. The date a joke between them now, something trotted out when they were drunk or miserable. His love life was as disastrous as hers, though – probably worse come to think of it. He had a habit of falling in love with straight guys. That never ended well. Wren couldn't understand it. Keegan was excessively handsome, six-foot six inches tall, a beautiful ebony Adonis. What man wouldn't snap him up?

Gracie began cleaning her fur, her mistress's pain all but forgotten. Sometimes she wished she could be a cat and put aside all her problems so easily. Maybe then she wouldn't feel so alone.

No career. No ambition. No boyfriend.

"Perhaps I should become a nun," she muttered.

HER FATHER PHONED JUST as she was getting ready for bed. She'd put on her pink fluffy robe and Kermit slippers, and her Kindle was switched on and ready. All she had to do now was cozy up under the sheets and wish she was anywhere but here.

Wren answered her cell with a sigh and said, "Dad, what is it?"

"The game tonight looks like it's going to be good," said her father, Warwick 'Wick' King. He sounded excited. "I think my team really have a good chance of winning!"

"That's good," she said, stifling a yawn. It was nice to hear her father happy, even if it meant potential trouble ahead. "How much money did you put on it?"

"Not much." He went silent for a while. "About two grand."

Wren was so glad she wasn't drinking hot chocolate at that moment, otherwise she would've spit it out all over her clean sheets. Her father had a gambling problem, or was quite possibly verging on having one. It wasn't serious, but every now and again he'd make a colossal mistake and end up losing a lot of money. She was worried about him, and her mother was tired of it. No wonder Mom spent so much time at her "friend" Anthony's house.

"What if they have a bad game?" she asked, trying to be practical. She tried to stroke Gracie, but she tried to bite her. Her cat didn't like being interrupted when she was having a bath. "Or what if the game gets called off because of the weather?"

"It won't," he assured her. He sounded *too* confident, like he didn't really believe his own words. "You have to have a little faith in these things."

"Dad..."

She loved her dad. She wanted to tell him that Mom was maybe having an affair and that his gambling was destroying his marriage, but she didn't want to make him unhappy. Her father was the jolliest person she knew, so much so that he dressed up as Santa Claus to visit the kids at the children's hospital every Christmas. Did she have the right to upset him? Did he deserve to know the truth?

"Are you dressing up as Santa this year?" she asked him. "You know how much you love that."

Yes, I know, I'm a coward, but I really shouldn't interfere with my parents' marriage. It's not any of my business.

"Of course," he said proudly. "I make a damn fine Santa if I do say so myself. Isn't it a bit early to start thinking about Christmas? I thought you'd be thinking about Halloween. It's only thirty days away. I can't wait for the best decorated house competition! I'm going to win for sure this year."

She laughed, remembering the years of her childhood when she'd really thought her dad was Santa Claus. Those were happy, innocent times. Wick often got carried away during the holidays, whether it was Christmas, Halloween, or Thanksgiving.

"And are you going to be one of my elves this year?" he asked.

He always asked, and she always said no. Her life was terrible enough as it was without prancing around like an idiot in green stockings for the whole world to see and laugh at.

"Maybe next year," she told him. They both knew it was a lie.

They talked a bit about what she'd been up today, which didn't take long, and then her dad hung up to feed the dog and get dinner ready. By now Wren was tired and not really into reading, but she really needed to update her friend Miranda on tonight's date of doom. She desperately needed to talk to someone about it. Keegan was on a night shift at the sheriff's office. She'd tell him about it over coffee tomorrow.

She opened her laptop and connected to Miranda. Her friend lived in Lake Como, Italy, and was probably just getting up for work now. Wren bet she'd been dying to know how her date went all night.

Miranda's face popped up on the screen. She had brown hair, freckles and a pretty face. It felt good to see her. Wren missed her a lot. They'd grown up together, but Miranda's family had moved to

Italy when she was fifteen. They'd kept in touch through letters, email, and now Skype, but it just wasn't the same. Wren hadn't been in the same room with her since she'd visited Italy four years ago.

"Haven't you gone to bed yet?" Miranda joked. She had a very mild Italian accent now, which Wren still found hard to get used to. It just reinforced the fact that her best friend was a world away.

"I'm not really sleepy," she told her.

Miranda grinned and said, "Go on! Tell me how the date went!"

Wren thought about telling her the truth, but it made her cringe over how she'd overreacted to the hint that he might want marriage in the future. They'd been through a lot together, and Miranda had stuck by her through thick and thin, but over this she was deeply embarrassed.

"It went okay," Wren lied. It felt like poison on her tongue. She hated lying to her best friend. "It wasn't something out of a romance novel, but we got on really well. We're going out again tonight."

"That's great!" Miranda declared. "I really am pleased for you."

They laughed and then the topic turned inevitably onto Miranda's twin daughters, Esme and Ella. They were the apple of her friend's eye. The girls were undeniably cute and she loved them to bits but it only cemented the fact even further that Wren had nothing.

"Esme and Ella want to know if their godmother is coming to their thirteenth birthday party in February," Miranda said. "I told them she was very busy and probably wouldn't have the time."

"I'd love to come, but I can't afford it at the moment."

Wren couldn't afford anything at the moment. Pretty soon she'd have to cancel her Wi-Fi and she loathed doing that. She knew she needed a job but she was not going to do any old crap again, especially after working at the terminally boring tourist office for so many years. There was something out there for her, a vocation or job or career that was perfect for her. She just had to find it.

"Beppe will pay for your airfare," Miranda told her. "He owes me."

"He said he wouldn't pay after last time..."

Miranda looked away from the screen for a second, a brief flicker of sadness, and said, "Like I said, he owes me. You're coming whether you like it or not."

Wren tried not to cry as she thanked her. It was such a generous thing to do, and it perked her night up no end. She couldn't wait to see her best friend face to face again. It would be just like old times.

"You could bring your new boyfriend as well," Miranda suggested.

Wren's face fell. She smiled politely and said, "Sure. I...I could do that."

Miranda started talking about something else, but by then Wren had already tuned her out. The brief delight of seeing her friend again had been soured by the fact that she was lying to her. She had no boyfriend and she never would. *I will die alone, with only a cat to eat me after I'm dead.*

Chapter 2

"WAKE UP!"

Wren ignored the strident, bossy voice. She didn't want to get up just yet. What was the point? She had no job and no life. When you had nothing, you clung onto what you did have, which were leisurely lie-ins, bad hair days, and cutting out pictures of attractive movie stars from magazines and sticking them in a picture book. She did have her trip to Italy to look forward to, but even that was tinged with dread because of all the lies she'd spun about her so-called boyfriend.

I could hire an actor to play my lover.

"Do I have to tip you out of bed?" the voice demanded. "I will do it you know. I'm not just a pretty face."

She opened her eyes, startled to find a woman in her bedroom. The woman was small, pudgy, but very pretty, with frizzy blonde hair down to her shoulders. She wore large framed red spectacles and she carried a clipboard in her hands. Aside from the white baggy dress she wore the only other distinguishing feature about her was her angel's wings.

"You look like an angel," Wren said dreamily.

She laughed. "That's because I am an angel."

"Did I suffocate in my sleep?" she demanded. "I'd always imagined I'd die by suffocating in my sleep."

The angel's white, creamy wings pulled back inside her body, and she said, "Hmm. You're quite dark this morning."

The angel wrote something down on her clipboard. Wren closed her eyes, willing this apparition to go away. *Maybe I'm so lonely and so pathetic that I'm imagining things now. Pretty soon I'll be howling at the moon and buying lotto tickets.*

"It's time to get your life into shape," shouted the angel, directly into her ear. She had a voice like an elephant marching band. "So, get your lazy ass out of bed!"

Wren ignored her. She wasn't real. Angels didn't exist.

"I will not take no for an answer," the so-called angel screamed. "I have never taken no for an answer and I'm not about to start now."

"Would you take 'get lost' for an answer instead then?" Wren said.

The angel pulled the covers back, grabbed hold of Wren's arm, and pulled her out of bed. She landed on the floor and felt one of her Kermit slippers touch her mouth. It tasted like feet.

Wren jumped to her feet, a little exasperated now, and said, "What is it you want from me?"

The angel smiled sweetly. "So, you don't think I'm a hallucination, then?"

"Perhaps not," Wren conceded. She was thoroughly wide awake now. "Though the jury's still out on that one. I've had a very bad decade."

"Then we can begin."

The angel nodded her head and vanished in a flash of feathers. Wren picked up one of the feathers, gloriously soft and white, but it disintegrated in her hands like it was made of cobwebs.

"Hello?" she called out.

The angel appeared to have gone. Or maybe she'd never really been there. *Am I still asleep? Am I dreaming?*

Wren's cell phone rang. She reached out to her bedside table and grabbed it. It was her mom. What was she doing calling so early?

"Mom?" she said, concerned. She rubbed her eyes, finding bits of sleep the size of tennis balls. "What is it?"

Dot sighed theatrically and said, "I've killed your father."

Wren sighed too. She'd obviously found out about the gambling. They'd probably been arguing all night. Those two could argue for the Olympics.

Wren sighed again and asked, "He told you, then?"

"I came back from my...friend's house last night and decided to go online and order a nice holiday. I've always wanted to go to Paris. I'm not that keen on the French, but I suppose it can't be helped. I dated this French exchange student at school once. He cheated on me with my best friend." She appeared thoughtful for a moment. "Of course, my card was declined and I phoned up the bank and was told our joint account had no money in it! At first, I thought that maybe my identity had been stolen. You remember my friend Delilah? A fat Russian gentleman called Petro stole her identity and opened up a cigar shop in Moscow. Poor Delilah was arrested and everything."

Wren waited for her Mom to get her breath back. When she started on a topic she could go on forever without stopping to even breathe.

Dot laughed. "Delilah and I can laugh about it now. Well, I can. She still breaks into tears whenever it gets brought up. Now, where was I? Oh yes. Your father is a scoundrel. I hate him. I wish I had killed him."

She heard pots and pans clanking downstairs, and then some type of glass smash. She hoped the cat wasn't jumping around the kitchen counters again. She liked to cause a mess when she could.

"Perhaps you and Dad should have a serious talk," Wren suggested. "Or maybe just a normal talk where you don't argue all the time."

"We did have a serious talk," said her mom. "Well, I talked and he sat there cowering like the coward he is. The thing is..."

Wren heard another crash downstairs. That did not sound like the antics of a mischievous cat. Was she being burgled?

"Mom, I have to go," she said, fearing the worst. "Talk to you later."

"But..."

She hung up and put on her dressing gown. There was no way she was going to confront a burglar in her nightie. If she was murdered she did not want to be examined by the police in moth eaten nightwear. How embarrassing would that be?

She grabbed a pink polka dot umbrella out of the umbrella stand in the hallway. She and Keegan had bought it from a small village while on one of their regular drives up the coast last year. It had sheltered them from quite a bad rainfall if she recalled.

"What the hell are you doing?" Wren cried out.

It was the crazy angel. She had half demolished her kitchen. Pots and pans were strewn across the floor and most of the fridge's contents were on the table. All the cupboard doors were wide open, and one of them was even half off its hinges. The angel herself was busy whisking eggs in a glass bowl using a fork.

"I'm making breakfast," the angel answered. She regarded the messy kitchen and shrugged, as if destroying Wren's house was of no consequence. "I think that's perfectly obvious, even to someone with bed hair as bad as yours."

"I do not have bad bed hair!" Wren screamed.

Wren looked in the mirror on the wall and almost cringed. She looked like she'd been bungee jumping after being dragged through a hedge backwards and mauled by big cats.

She tried to control her breathing. She didn't think she'd ever been so angry in all her life. She would've preferred burglars.

"Why are you making my breakfast?" Wren asked.

"You don't eat healthy enough," the angel replied. "Do you like omelets?"

"I prefer my oatmeal thank you very much," she told her. "Besides, eggs give me gas."

The petite apparition ignored her, continuing to whisk away as if Wren weren't even in the room. She marched over to the angel and snatched the fork out of her hand. She looked up at her with eyes so venomous Wren was actually a little scared.

"Give me that fork back," the angel demanded.

"Tell me what you're doing here first," Wren said.

She stood up to face her, but her eyes only reached Wren's chin. She may have been short, but she was about as intimidating as a pit-bull.

"I've been sent to sort your life out," the angel explained.

"My life doesn't need sorting out," Wren said.

The angel crossed her arms. "Really? You have no job and no lover. You have no life. Your cat may be very cute but that hardly constitutes a meaningful relationship."

"It does to me," Wren said defensively.

"The people upstairs obviously think something is wrong or otherwise I wouldn't be here."

Wren didn't want to argue with her, but she had no choice.

"I'm going to Italy in February," she said smugly. "People who don't have lives do not go to Italy."

"And who did you tell your friend you were going with, hmm?" said the angel, her smugness equally as smug. "Face it, sister, your life is a train wreck and a car crash combined and it needs sorting out pretty quick." She smiled giddily and said, "Do you like bacon bits in your omelet? I bet you do! I'll add them in anyway, just to make sure."

Wren wanted to scream in frustration. The angel was making a mess of her kitchen. One look at the eggshells on the floor and Wren's decision was made for her. She marched over, grabbed the bowl out of the woman's hands, and tipped the contents into the sink. The angel looked at her like she'd just gunned down her mother.

"That was cruel," snapped the angel. She looked like she was going to cry. At the moment Wren didn't care. She just wanted rid of her.

"Get out," Wren commanded, sounding a lot like her mother when she was in one of her moods. "Get out before I call the police!"

The angel looked at her with quivering lips and said, "But I'm here to help you."

"I don't need any help," Wren insisted.

The angel's sad face was enough to thaw even the hardest of hearts. Wren ignored her, and with a pop and a bang she was gone.

I must've drunk more than I imagined last night.

IT TOOK HER HALF AN hour to clean up the angel's mess, though Gracie did help by licking up the spilled eggs on the kitchen tiles. Wren still didn't believe what she'd seen. The angel was obviously real, and yet she still couldn't admit to herself that she existed. It would mean the universe was far bigger than she ever imagined it could be.

Gracie sat by her feet and looked up at her with adorable eyes. She picked her up and said, "You saw her too, right?"

Gracie meowed. She took that as a yes.

THERE WAS A TEXT MESSAGE waiting for her on her cell after she'd gotten out of the shower. It was from Cedric. She was going to ignore it, but figured she at least ought to read what it said. The message read, *"Maybe we can try again some time? Call me."*

Wren deleted the text. There was no way she was going on a date with Cedric ever again. She still couldn't believe she'd actually gone out with him in the first place. She must've been mad and desperate.

There was a frantic knocking at the front door as she dried her hair.

"I'm coming!" she shouted, rushing down the stairs as fast as possible. "I'm coming!"

She opened the door to find her dad. His cheeks were red and his eyes looked tired. He'd probably spent the night sleeping in his garden.

He sighed and hung his head in shame. "I need to ask you something."

She let him in and told him to sit down while she made them both a cup of coffee. Wren wasn't in the mood for this right now. What with the date and the angel, her life was getting complicated enough. The last thing she needed was to get involved in her parents' marriage. That always led to disaster. She'd suggested once that they get a divorce and they didn't speak to her for a month.

"There you go," she said, handing her dad a mug of hot coffee. "Tell me if you need more milk."

He drank some and sighed happily. "You could always make tea and coffee perfectly. Why is that?"

Wren shrugged and said, "It's a gift."

"What did you put in it? Nutmeg?"

"Just a dash."

He drank some more coffee while she waited for him to get to the reason why he was here. Not that her father needed a reason to visit her, but usually he always had ulterior motives.

Gracie jumped on his lap and he started stroking her. Her fur was wet. She'd obviously been for a run around in the rain. Wren always liked the smell of wet cat for some reason. It reminded her of spring storms.

"Has Mom thrown you out?" she asked him, sitting at the table.

"I wouldn't blame her if she did," said Dad. He took a sip of his coffee and sighed with pleasure. "I did something stupid and I'm not proud of it. I was sure I was on to a good thing."

"You have to stop this," she advised him. "Please."

He looked at her sharply. "Do you think I'm an addict?"

"I think...possibly," she admitted. "Maybe you're on your way to becoming one."

It looked like she was going to become involved in her parent's marriage whether she liked it or not. Those two stubborn old fools never listened to advice, but she was going to give them some anyway. Maybe they'd take notice, or maybe they'd ignore her. It was up to them.

"You need to talk to her," she told him. "You need to sit her down and really talk to her. You can explain your problem. I'm sure she'll listen."

"What problem?" he asked. He looked confused.

Wren sighed. This was like pulling thorns from a rose stem. Until her father realized he had a problem there would be no telling him. In the meantime, she had an appointment she had to keep.

"Stay here until I get back," she ordered him.

He continued to stroke the cat as he said, "Fine. It's comfortable here."

She left him to it as she went to get dressed. While she didn't have a job or a life or a boyfriend, she still had commitments, even though those commitments could drain even the sanest man of their soul. The unemployment office beckoned...

Chapter 3

The local unemployment office was a building constructed in the seventies, made from concrete and hopelessness. It was drabber than a mental asylum and just as mentally exhausting. Once you entered its grey confines, your spirits were sapped and your confidence battered like a car stuck on the train tracks. It was, literally, hell on earth.

The journey from her tiny little village on the coast to the city took an hour. She wasn't sure it was worth it to enter a building that made her feel so small, but for now, she needed the unemployment checks.

The unemployment office woman looked at her with contempt and said, "Have you been looking for jobs this week?"

They both knew the answer to that question. Wren hadn't been looking for a job because there was nothing that she wanted to do. Until she figured out what her vocation in life was, she would do something about it.

Wren smiled and said, "Of course. I've written many, many job application letters. It's only a matter of time."

The unemployment office woman, Maureen, sighed, and said, "Time is all we have. It's always ticking away, stealing our life, until we end up old and alone."

Wren had always feared ending up old and alone. Perhaps she and Maureen could share a flat together with their fifty cats and moan about lost loves and ask the eternal question; when did it all go wrong?

Wren looked behind her, at the lines of depressed people waiting to see someone. There wasn't a happy face among them.

"See you next week then," said Maureen.

"Bye," said Wren.

She exited the unemployment office with less hope than on previous occasions. The angel had made her feel even worse about herself. As if she needed someone to magically appear in her house and tell her that her life was terrible. She knew her life was terrible.

SHE STOPPED BY THE Metropolis, a cute little coffee house in the center of Snowflake Bay. She liked it in there. It was all silvery and shiny like the inside of a spaceship and the beautiful baristas always treated her like she was a VIP. She loved the exotic flavors of all their various coffees, and they made a mean strawberry and cream scone.

"The usual?" the cute male barista asked. He was six-foot, with a scruffy brown beard and piercing blue eyes. He was the epitome of handsome and he made her visits worthwhile.

I do not have a crush on him.

"Thank you, Jordan," Wren said, trying not to blush.

He talked to her while waiting for the water to boil. "My last term at college starts in a few weeks. I'm kind of nervous."

"You'll do fine," she assured him.

Jordan was studying law. He'd told her all about his ambition to help the small people, those who couldn't afford high-priced lawyers and were shafted by the system. He had a noble goal and a career in mind, and she envied him that. Wren would miss him when he left.

I do not have a crush on him.

"Let's hope my replacement is as nice to customers as I am," he said as he poured her coffee.

"Your father could never find someone as good as you," she told him.

Jordan's father, Garrett Knowles, owned the Metropolis. He was a good man, though she didn't know him that well, even though his family had lived in Snowflake Bay for almost as long as her own. Perhaps the town wasn't as small as she thought. Or maybe she just didn't care to know everyone so intimately.

He blushed and said, "Thanks."

She took her coffee and strawberry cream scone to a small table by the window. She ate and drank and watched the world go by outside. Everyone was in such a hurry to get somewhere. What was so important? Why didn't she have something important to rush to, something she couldn't miss?

She thought about Miranda. That was something to look forward to. She had to tell her the truth about Cedric first, though. That would be painful. She and Miranda had made a pact to never lie to each other. Wren had broken that pact. She knew she'd forgive her, but that didn't mean it was okay.

"What are you thinking about?" the angel asked.

Where had she come from? She hadn't seen her sit down. She didn't dare think that she just appeared out of nowhere, because then she'd have to believe that she was a real angel and not a stalker.

"I'm thinking about throwing my coffee all over you and making a run for it," Wren told her, unable to hide her smirk.

She smiled sweetly from her seat opposite and said, "That would be wrong. I might be scolded."

Wren sighed and began eating her scone. Whipped cream dripped down her chin, making a mess, but she ignored it.

"How did you find me?" Wren asked her.

"I always know where to find you," the angel answered.

"Try saying that without sounding like a creepy stalker," she told her.

The angel sighed and began eating a large chocolate chip cookie. The snack had just seemed to appear in her hands. Had she used magic to make it come to being, or had it been in her pocket all along?

She really is an angel...

"Do you really want to know what I'm thinking about?" Wren asked. She thought she'd have a little fun at the angel's expense.

The angel smiled, still eating, and nodded her head.

Wren sighed heavily. "I was thinking about the angel that invaded my home last night, and how stupid she looks in that dress of hers."

The angel choked on her cookie and Wren burst out laughing. She looked at Wren crossly and vanished, the half-eaten cookie falling onto the floor.

Wren couldn't deny it anymore. The woman really was an angel. Well, either that or she had access to teleportation technology, and why would someone with such advanced technology want to pretend to be an angel and mess with her?

"I wish people would clean up after themselves," said Jordan, bending over to clean up the broken cookie. "I've had enough today what with Veronica's ranting and railing outside."

Wren's eyes were instantly drawn to his perfect bottom as it pressed tightly against his jeans.

Well, fine, I have a little crush on him. What's the harm in it?

"Veronica Van Clark?" Wren queried. "She's just opened up that coffee shop down the road. I tried it. The place is a dump."

He turned to her, dustpan and brush in his hands, and said, "She was waiting outside when I opened up, accusing Dad of breaking into her store and sabotaging her espresso machine. All her customers had the runs or something. She was hysterical."

"She does like to make a scene."

Veronica was always the lead in the Snowflake Bay Amateur Dramatics productions, and she overacted marvelously. Wren didn't know anyone in town who hadn't had cause to cross words with the woman. She could get riled up if you so much as looked at her sideways.

"I'm going to miss this place when I leave," Jordan admitted.

"We'll miss you too," she told him, trying to hold back her drool. She really would miss him, and her silly little fantasies of him.

He smiled wickedly and said, "I think I'll miss you the most." He winked at her and walked away.

"What the..."

She looked back at him, but he was too busy talking with the only other barista in the place, Aarna. She seemed more his type. The girl was his own age, with the exotic looks of a Bollywood star. Quite why Aarna wasn't already a model, but working in a café she wasn't entirely sure.

He winked at me! Oh god, he winked at me...

"Why do you look like you just saw Chris Pratt naked?" Keegan asked, sitting down in the angel's previously vacated seat.

She grinned and said, "I'll tell you later."

Wren told him straight away, of course. She could hardly keep such news to herself for long. Keegan grinned, enjoying the story, staring back at Jordan as he talked with his father behind the counter. Garrett was handsome too, sort of like what Jordan would look like in twenty years' time.

And that boy is going to age very well.

"Why are all the cute ones straight?" said Keegan with a sigh.

"Am I in with a shot here?" she asked. "Or am I being naïve?"

"I honestly don't know," Keegan admitted. He smiled and rubbed his deputy's badge of imaginary dust. "But you need to take a chance. By the way, how did the date with the window guy go? He's sitting over there, by the way."

She hadn't noticed Cedric when she came in. He was sitting at a table by himself, nursing a large frothy coffee. His mind seemed elsewhere.

Did I do that? Did I make him miserable?

Wren went through the story once again in painful detail. Every time she relived it, she felt more stupid.

"Maybe I was too harsh," Wren admitted. She watched Jordan as he stood at the side of the counter, talking animatedly on his cell phone. He seemed quite agitated. "He could turn out to be a great guy with a boring job. I might have just missed out on having a happy ever after."

Keegan shook his head. "When he came to do a job at the sheriff's station, he bored me to tears with his story about double glazing. You had a lucky escape there."

Wren was cross. "You could've told me he was boring."

"You needed a date, even if it was with a man who could make a statue fall to sleep."

They heard raised voices behind the counter. Jordan and his father were arguing quite heatedly. The other barista, Aarna, was hastily making an exit. She'd obviously witnessed this kind of behavior before and wanted to stay out of it. Wren, however, had never seen either of them angry before. They always seemed so calm.

"That looks brutal," said Wren.

"I hate it when pretty people fight," said Keegan.

Wren gasped as Jordan punched his father. It was a rather half-hearted attempt, but it did the trick. Jordan looked contrite for a moment before running around the counter and out of the café.

I have to do something.

She ran to Garrett, pulling a wad of tissues from her purse. As he dabbed the blood pouring from his nose, she noticed an impatient customer at the counter and a milk heating machine about to overheat.

Shit.

She grabbed a large silver coffee mug and shoved it under the nozzle before the hot milk could spill everywhere. She sighed with contention. Hot milk was a favorite of hers.

"I asked for just a simple milky coffee," the customer complained.

Wren smiled sweetly and looked to Garrett for what to do. She'd worked in a coffee shop many moons ago but she didn't want to be seen to be interfering. Then again...

She moved the mug to the coffee machine, selecting ordinary coffee. It poured into the milk and she mixed it by hand with a spoon. It smelled divine yet there was something missing.

"Do you mind if I put a smidgen of cinnamon in here?" Wren asked the customer. Garrett was sitting on a small stool now, watching her with curiosity. "You won't regret it."

The moody customer, an Asian lady with a cute kitten cut, said, "Fine. Whatever."

Wren sprinkled a dash of cinnamon onto the coffee and handed it to the customer. She took a sip and smiled in pleasure.

"That's lovely!" the woman declared.

"I make a mean cup of coffee," said Wren smugly.

The customer smiled and took her drink to a table. Wren was about to serve another customer when she spotted Veronica Van Clark enter the premises. She grinned and walked up to the counter. She tapped the next customer, local gardener and president of the knitting club, Mrs. Wanda Ivory, on the shoulder.

"Can I help you?" Wanda asked grandly.

Wanda Ivory was ninety-two years old, but after a lifetime of eating well and keeping fit she looked sixty. She was stern, with jet black dyed hair, and wore the latest fashions to come out of New York. She had more grandchildren and great grandchildren than you could shake a stick at. Everyone adored and respected her. Even Wren, once upon a time, had found herself asking the treasured old woman for advice. Wanda Ivory *was* Snowflake Bay.

"Why risk drinking the slop they serve here?" Veronica asked. Her tone was polite, but anyone could see the spite and venom underneath. "They probably haven't cleaned their equipment in years."

"I always drink in here," Wanda protested.

"You could..."

Wren had had enough. "Veronica, please leave. Poaching customers here is a dastardly thing to do."

Veronica glared daggers at Wren before pouting and leaving.

"That woman needs a good rogering," said Wanda.

Wren burst into laughter. "You have a dirty mind, Wanda."

She served the town matriarch, who sipped her coffee and smiled dreamily. She pushed a hefty ten-dollar note into the tips jar and winked at Wren before she sat down at a table to enjoy her drink.

Keegan gave her the thumbs up as he walked up to the counter.

"Are you working here now?" Keegan asked. "Because as an officer of the law I should tell you that we get freebies here."

Wren smirked. "No, you do not."

"Anyway, I just got a call. There's been another burglary. That's the third business that's been robbed in town in the past two weeks."

Wren smiled as Keegan exited the coffee shop. He may not have seemed your typical deputy sheriff, but he was good at his job. It didn't hurt that Keegan's father was the sheriff himself. The man had wanted his son to follow in his footsteps as a police officer and had despaired of it ever happening when his son came out as gay. Everyone, including Keegan, was surprised when he revealed he still wanted to be a cop. Even Wren had had to put aside her stereotypical views of gay men only being hairdressers and wedding planners.

She shook off thoughts of Keegan and turned back to Garrett. He was staring out of the window. Jordan was sitting at one of the rarely used outside tables.

"Are you okay?" Wren asked him.

"I'm fine," Garrett snapped.

"Do you want to talk about it?"

He shook his head. "I'm fine. There's no need to fuss."

Wren reigned her anger in, knowing the man was just upset and taking it out on her. She stormed back to her table and sat with her back to him. It was too cold to go outside at the moment. When she looked out the window Jordan was just walking past. Their eyes met for a brief second and he grinned at her.

"I'm sorry," said Garret, walking up to her. "I shouldn't take out my problems on you."

She smiled with sympathy. "It was none of my business."

"Can you...keep serving while I change?" he asked. There was blood all over his shirt. "Rob bought me this shirt."

He was referring to Sheriff Rob Fisher. Why would he buy Garrett a shirt?

"I'd call Aarna back, but she gets triggered by other people arguing," Garret added. "And I need to call the caterers for a dinner party my wife's hosting." He smiled." It's going to be an epic party."

Wren hesitated, not sure what to say. She didn't want to work in a coffee shop. It was too hot and clammy.

But the joy on that woman's face when I served her coffee with cinnamon was priceless. I made her happy!

She shrugged. "I suppose."

He smiled and headed into the back room. Wren took a deep breath. She could do this. Making coffee wasn't hard. The coffee machine looked complicated, but she'd worked similar ones before. This would be a walk in the park.

A familiar woman walked up the counter. She was tall, with pouty lips and a blonde wig. She was trying to look young but only managed to make herself look her age, which was obviously knocking on fifty.

"What can I get you?" Wren asked, putting on her sweetest, happiest voice.

"Where's my husband?" the woman demanded. Her voice was gravelly, like she'd smoked forty a day since she was a toddler.

Wren grinned. "Katie..."

This woman was Garret's wife. She hadn't recognized her straight away because she'd obviously had some form of cosmetic surgery. It didn't do her any favors. Her face looked like it was melting.

"He's in the back getting changed," Wren explained. "Jordan punched him."

Katie sighed. "This is all getting out of hand. I didn't want it to come out like this."

The woman sighed and went to confront her husband. Wren tried to ignore her curiosity about what was going on, but it was difficult. Half an hour passed as she served customers and heard shouting coming from the back room. She couldn't tell what was being said, but it was impressive. Something had clearly upset the entire family this morning.

"Sorry, we're all out of scones," Wren told a devastated customer. Garret's scones always sold out very quickly. Wren could live off them for the rest of her life she loved them so much.

"What the..." Cedric exited the bathroom, watching her. She hadn't realized he was still here.

Is he spying on me? Have I got a stalker?

Wren knew she should be concerned but Cedric seemed harmless enough. He was a boring man who led a boring life. He was probably just working up the courage to ask her out on another date. It was sweet, really.

"Do you work here?" Cedric asked nervously.

"Not really," said Wren. "Can I... can I get you anything?"

He shook his head. "I really have to go."

He almost ran out of the place. Wren had to smile. He was acting very shy and insecure around her. Had she made that big of an impression last night?

Maybe I'm more desirable than I thought.

The idea that someone, even someone as dull as Cedric, found her attractive, boosted her confidence just a little bit.

There was a loud crash in the back room. It sounded like someone had been pushed into a pile of boxes.

Maybe she should see what was wrong. What if the argument had evolved into an actual physical altercation? Garret was a big man. What if he hurt his wife?

Katie stormed out of the back room, followed by Garret's words, "You can sleep at your mothers!"

"You really are pig headed," Katie snapped back, exiting the café. Her face was red, her cheeks puffy from crying. "Pig headed and *mean!*"

Wren didn't know where to look, and neither did any of the customers. It felt like they'd all waded into some sort of theatre show about the dissolution of a marriage. It was intimate and very, very embarrassing.

Garret emerged from the back room in a clean white shirt. He sighed and walked up to Wren.

"I can take over now," he said. "Thank you for this."

"Are you okay?" she asked.

He shrugged. "Who knows?"

Chapter 4

Jordan flitted through her mind in various stages of undress as she left the coffee shop. He was clearly in love with her. She hadn't been imagining it. He had winked at her suggestively, right? He wanted her.

No way! There's no way someone as young and fit as him could ever fancy someone over fifteen years older than he was. I'm old and ugly and have at least three grey hairs at last count. He must be playing me.

But what if he really did want her? Could she really pass up on the chance of making out with someone who made Chris Hemsworth look like a troll that had just been beaten to a pulp with the ugly stick?

She needed someone to confide in.

"Who's Jordan again?" Maureen asked.

Wren sighed. Maureen at the unemployment office had been the only person she could think of to talk to at that moment in time. Miranda would be dealing with the kids' post-school and she didn't want to disturb her, and Keegan was off investigating his burglary. Maureen would have to do for the moment. She seemed to be the kind of person who lived off other people's drama, judging by the *Days of Our Lives* calendar on her desk.

"He works in Metropolis, a coffee shop in Snowflake Bay," Wren told her again. The woman had the attention span of a geriatric goldfish. "You must know him. You live in Snowflake Bay, right? You could hardly forget those buns."

"Oh yes," said Maureen, smiling. Her huge nose twitched like a rabbit staring down a carrot. "I know him, and his buns are delicious. I get crumbs all over the place!"

Either she was trying really hard with her euphemisms or she was actually talking about edible buns. Wren realized it was the latter.

"He winked at me," Wren confessed, playing with her hair, nervous. At the moment it was frizzy and mousy brown and a tangled mess of split ends. "I'm not sure what it means. What do you think it means?"

"He might have glaucoma," Maureen suggested.

"He's only twenty-one," Wren reminded her.

Maureen crossed her arms and said, "My uncle started going bald when he was five, and I know of a woman who had a baby in her sixties. This world is odd. Look at your hair for example."

"What...what's wrong with my hair?"

Maureen sighed audibly. Wren could see a giant mole on the woman's neck and the thick, tiny hair that sprouted from it. The mole was mocking her. She hated that mole and everything it stood for. The mole was evil.

"Do you want me to be honest?" Maureen asked her.

Wren had a feeling that Maureen was going to be very blunt. She suddenly didn't want to hear this. The angel had been bad, but Maureen was going to be vicious.

"Maureen, I..."

"You don't use conditioner. You don't comb your hair. You look like a murder victim."

Wren gasped and said, "Listen, Maureen..."

She was about to shout at her and call her out on her own murder victim hair when she noticed something. Sitting at another booth and talking animatedly to another unemployment office worker was the angel. She was dressed in a sharp black business suit and her hair was tied up in a bun. When she saw Wren was looking her way she smiled, waved, and continued talking.

"Who's that?" Wren asked Maureen, pointing to the angel.

"I've never seen her before," said Maureen. "What does she have to do with this weird barista you think fancies you?"

Wren sighed and said, "Nothing. Look, I better go. It was nice talking to you, Maureen. You were...refreshing."

Maureen smiled genuinely, blushed and said, "You're welcome."

She eyed the angel as she left, almost walking into people in the process. What was she doing there, dressed like that? Was she spying on her or was she also out of a job and looking for work?

Did out of work angels get unemployment benefits?

"Got you," Wren exclaimed, grabbing the angel's arm as she exited the building. She looked at her in surprise.

"Are you following me?" Wren asked her.

"Believe it or not, I have more than one client," said the angel primly. Her sharp business suit made her breasts heave spectacularly. "And they're not all as hostile as you."

"Oh." Wren felt a little embarrassed. "Sorry. So...how is it going?"

The angel grinned and said, "Damian is quite picky when it comes to finding his one true love. He has confidence issues. But I think I've found him someone truly special. Only now I have to accidentally set them up. That can be quite tricky, especially when you don't have nearly as much magic as some of the other higher-up angels. Just because they have a god or goddess for a parent, they think they're *sooo* special."

"So, you're a cupid as well as a...life fixer-upper person?"

The angel's smile was wide and multi-dimensional. "As far as I'm concerned, both jobs compliment the other, and some people require...extra work."

Wren mulled over her words, about magic and gods and goddesses. What gods and goddesses were those? Was she pulling her leg, or was she deadly serious? Wren knew she was angel, so that meant there were other things out there that would probably rock her world too.

"Anyway, I better get home," Wren said, feeling awkward now. The angel was smiling at her expectantly. "I need to...feed the cat."

The angel held her hand out. "I'm Fiona by the way. I probably should've introduced myself last night."

"Probably," Wren mumbled.

Fiona smiled awkwardly and said, "So..."

Wren shook her hand and said, "Pleased to meet you. So...goodbye."

Wren hurried off down the street, just in case Fiona tried to follow her. She had no doubt that the angel could use her magic or whatever to track her down like a pint-sized blonde Terminator, but

at the moment, she just wanted to put some space between them and
think.

Chapter 5

Wren didn't believe in anything. She never had. Her parents weren't churchgoers, though her father's father was Jewish, and she'd never even thought about god or religion before. She may have offered up a prayer to whatever deity might be listening during the dark days with Alex, but that was her sole experience with such matters. If angels existed, and gods and goddesses, what did that mean?

Should I pray now? Would that help?

She unlocked her front door and picked up the post. It was nothing but bills. She always paid her bills on time, so they were never a worry. She was fussy like that. Her mother had once forgotten to pay the electricity bill when she was about nine or ten. She could still remember the cries of horror when the TV went off and Dad missed the end of a football game.

"Hi sweetie," said Dad.

Wren almost jumped out of her skin. She'd forgotten he was still here. He must've been waiting for her to come back from the unemployment office all morning.

"I thought you'd left," Wren said, flopping down in her comfy chair. She noticed Dad had gotten cookie crumbs all over the couch.

"I thought I'd stick around until you got back," said Dad, lounging around as if he owned the place. He had even taken his socks off. "Thought we could have a nice long talk."

"That...would be nice."

Wren sighed and ran into the kitchen, eager to be away from him for a blissful moment. Something was going on with her dad other than the gambling and Mom chucking him out, she was sure of it. She wanted to help him, she really did, but he could make things so difficult sometimes.

She put some nibbles into Gracie's food bowl before noticing the cat flap on the back door was half open. Sometimes it froze like that in bad weather.

Wren opened the back door. Her back garden was quite spacious, mostly lawn, but with a large patio under a wooden gazebo near the back. It required very little maintenance, which suited her just fine. Gardening was not her forte, though when she'd first bought the house, she'd tried to give the place a colorful, floral makeover. It hadn't gone well.

Gracie sat on the small table under the gazebo with two other cats. One was ginger and the other was pure black. Wren thought she recognized the black one, though the ginger cat didn't ring any bells.

"Are you hungry?" Wren called.

All three cats turned to her, their watchful eyes boring into her soul. Wren was a little startled. There was something very sinister about it, like she'd caught them plotting world domination or something.

Are they plotting world domination?

Gracie ignored her and turned back to her friends. Wren decided to leave them to it. If she wanted to stay out in the cold, then it was up to her. Besides, it was time to bite the bullet and talk to her father. If it got him out of her hair and back into Mom's house, then so much the better.

"So," she said, sitting down next to him. "What do you want to talk about?"

He looked at his bitten nails, then at the ceiling, and then finally at his daughter. Wren suddenly started to fear the worst. Was he ill, or dying? Did he only have a week to live? Did he need a kidney?

"Say something," Wren urged him. "You're making me nervous."

"Remember...remember that bet I told you about last night?"

She nodded. She knew she should see what was coming but she didn't have a clue.

He said, "I used up the money we'd saved up to go on your mother's dream holiday, and your mother is very angry with me."

"I know that," said Wren.

He appeared surprised but carried on anyway. "The thing is...I didn't lose all that money. I won over a hundred grand."

Wren could barely digest his words. "One hundred thousand dollars?"

He nodded. "I think it was the happiest moment of my life. Not counting marrying your mom and your birth, of course."

She had this sudden image of her parents swimming in a pool full of bank notes. She jumped in after them, doing the breaststroke, fifty-dollar bills splashing into the air.

"Why is Mom angry then?" she asked. "You could take her anywhere she wanted with that amount of money."

He looked at his nails again. He always did that when he was being shifty.

"I was on a roll," he said. "I couldn't lose. I had to know whether I could win more."

Oh no. Please tell me he didn't...

"I took my winnings and went to a private poker game," Dad continued. His hands were trembling. "I was doing good at first, but...I bombed. I lost all the money."

Wren patted him on the shoulder. "You should've just..."

"I've not finished yet." He actually started to smile, as if it was one huge practical joke. "I needed to win Mom's holiday savings back, and so I borrowed some money. I lost that too."

Now they were getting to the crux of the matter. He wasn't here to unburden himself of his guilt or ask for advice. He only wanted money.

"I know you still have the money you got when you sued the tourist office, and..."

Wren laughed, cutting him off midsentence. He really had no idea. He thought she was loaded!

"I used that money to buy the house," Wren said. "I thought I told you that."

He looked at her, terrified. "You never told me that. I would remember if you'd told me that!"

"Dad, I have no money. Why do you think I'm collecting unemployment checks?"

He threw the cat off his knee and stormed to the door. He gave her a look that said she'd disappointed him, and it cut her deep.

No. It's not disappointment. He's scared.

"You really have no money?" he asked. "Really? You got nearly a million dollars from the settlement."

"I bought this house, and paid off yours and Mom's mortgage, and I went on all the holidays I wanted," she told him, worried now. "I got myself the most expensive health insurance for the rest of my life. I have about a grand left in savings. You can have that."

"It's not enough. It's not nearly enough."

He actually looked scared, though he was trying his hardest not to show it. She didn't like to see her father like this. He was supposed to be brave. He'd been a rock during the dark days. She never would've gotten through it without his love and support.

"Will you be okay?" she asked him.

He smiled. "Don't worry about me, sweetie. I can work my way out of this mess. I always know what to do."

"If you need my help for anything else you only have to ask."

He kissed her on the forehead and said, "I know that."

He left, leaving her desperately concerned about him. She wasn't sure whom exactly he owed money to, but she doubted it was someone who would forget such a large debt in a hurry.

Chapter 6

Wren had the most absurd dreams that night. She dreamed she owed money to an angel with raven black wings and a mad frown. The angel chased her around the unemployment office until she gave in and spat five-dollar bills out of her mouth like a machine gun. Then a naked Jordan walked in, called her an idiot, and stormed out again, saying he was going to be with someone who wasn't stupid. It was bizarre and silly and she couldn't get it out of her head.

"What do you think it means?" she asked her cat.

Her faithful feline yawned and went back to sleep. She wished she could sleep that easily. Oh, to be a cat...

She looked at her cell phone, sitting on her bedside table. She knew she should call her mother and tell her about the trouble Dad was in. She could sort it out. Her mother sorted everything out apart from the cracks in her own marriage. A loan shark would quiver at her mother's heels!

She dialed the number quickly but received no answer. This was odd in itself. Her mother always answered the phone for fear she was missing out on something important. Was she dead? Had she been kidnapped?

I have to go around there, don't I?

She dressed quickly in her hardly ever used running clothes and made her way around to her mother's house as quickly as possible. There didn't seem to be any signs of a fire, or a burglary, or a terrorist attack. In fact, all seemed quite calm.

"I bet she was on the john," she muttered to herself.

She was still worried, though, so she knocked politely on the door and waited for a response.

"Hello?" the man asked.

Wren looked at the man who had answered her mother's door up and down for a second. He was in his late forties, with silver hair and a cheeky smile. He was also stark naked.

"Who...who are you?" Wren asked.

Stop looking at it...

Stop looking at it...

The man grinned brazenly and said, "I'm Anthony. Who are you?"

"I'm the daughter of the people who live in this house."

His face fell like a deflating soufflé. His face started to go red, he panicked, and he slammed the door in her face. Wren waited for a few seconds before heading inside.

"Mom?" she called. "Dad?"

She went into the living room. All seemed suburban and normal.

"Mom?" she called again.

"Wren!" her mother shouted, sticking her head out of the kitchen. "What are you doing here?"

"Why are you naked in the kitchen?"

Her mother blushed, and Wren charged in to see what was wrong. She had an awful feeling that her mother was going senile, though that didn't explain the naked man who had answered the door.

"There's some things I have to explain to you," her mother muttered, sounding embarrassed. She indicated the naked man, now covering his manhood with his hands. "This is Anthony."

"We've met," said Wren, trying not to blush herself.

Her mother grinned and said, "He's my lover."

Wren figured she was the butt of a very sick joke, and mockingly looked around for a hidden camera. In her heart she knew it was no joke. She'd suspected that her mother's new friend was more than just a friend for a while now. To see and hear the truth in such an unashamed fashion was just too much to comprehend.

"Are you going to say something?" her mother asked. "Or would you like a cup of tea to calm you down first?"

"I'm perfectly calm and stable," said Wren.

"Then let's have a cup of tea anyway!"

As Wren's mother switched the kettle on Wren sat by the kitchen table, still too stunned to utter a word.

"Where's Dad?" Wren asked.

"I threw him out last night."

Wren sighed. "And you moved your lover straight in. Perfect. Was even Dad's side of the bed cold yet?"

"Your father has been sleeping on the sofa for...for months now. We've not been doing good."

Wren laughed. "Of course, you're not doing good. You're sleeping with another man."

Her mother sat by the table as the kettle boiled, forgotten. She was still naked. Neither of them were in a tea mood any longer.

Dot cleared her throat and said, "I met Anthony at my Spanish class."

"You don't go to Spanish classes."

"It was after your father forgot our wedding anniversary and spent the day at the bookies. I was angry. I decided I wanted to do something for me." She smiled at Anthony. He gave her a saucy wink and giggled. Wren wanted to throw up. "So, I found this local college prospectus, closed my eyes, and picked a course out at random. I ended up with Spanish."

Wren saw the sadness in her mother's eyes and decided to give her the benefit of the doubt. She was her mother and she loved her, no matter what.

"What happened?" Wren asked.

Her mother smiled and said, "There was this man that took my breath away. He complimented me and sent me gifts and told me how beautiful I was. How was I to resist? As your father spiraled ever deeper into gambling, I ended up further in Anthony's embraces. I love your father, don't get me wrong. I'll always love him. But I just can't live with him any longer."

"I know he's a character, but..."

"He pawned my wedding ring so he could bet on a horse, Wren. He used our holiday money to bet on a dog. He sold our TV to buy a hundred lottery scratch cards, none of which won him anything. I've had enough."

Wren took her mother's hand. "I understand completely. Maybe inviting Anthony to live here was a..."

Her mother laughed. "He's not living here. I just invited him over to comfort me. I'm not living with any man again."

They sat and drank their tea and talked about trivial things for a while, like what happened on the soaps yesterday, and global warming, and how their local council members were morons. It always felt a little odd to chat with her mother like they were best friends, but it also felt good. She liked the relationship they had, and she wouldn't change it for the world. She just wished her mother had been honest with her since the beginning.

"What about you?" her mother asked. She was *still* naked. "Is there anything in the romance department for you, or have you forgotten what a man's doo-dah looks like?"

"I know what a man's doo-dah looks like," said Wren, hating that particular euphemism. It was so elementary school. "I got a good look at Anthony's when he answered the door. It nearly poked my eye out."

Her mother blushed. "He knows how to use it too."

"I DON'T WANT TO KNOW!"

They laughed, and Wren said, "I'm going to die a spinster. I think I'm okay with that. Well, I'm about ninety percent okay with that. I only went out with Cedric the other night because I didn't want to upset you. I regretted it the moment the appetizers were served."

"I don't believe that," her mother snapped, suddenly angry. "I will not allow my daughter to die alone! Besides, I want grandchildren. Who else could I harvest organs from if one of mine were to fail?"

Wren stood up. They were back to the grandchildren thing again. She didn't want to hear this. It just upset them both in the end.

"I know you can't have children by natural means," said her mother kindly. "I've accepted that. I know you have too. But there are lots of other ways. I want you to be happy, love."

"Mom..."

"Do you want children, Wren?"

Wren pondered the question seriously before bidding her mother goodbye. As she opened the front door she heard Anthony calling to her from the top of the stairs. She looked up to find him fully clothed in a smart business suit. The transformation was uncanny. He looked like a banker.

"Sorry," said Wren. "I didn't recognize you with your clothes on."

He laughed sheepishly and said, "Try not to be too hard on her. She's been through a lot."

"I know that," said Wren. "While I accept your...relationship, it doesn't mean that I like it."

"We're just having a bit of fun," said Anthony. "There's nothing wrong with that."

"How do you think my dad feels?"

Anthony watched her sharply before saying, "I don't care about your father. I care about your mother. Her happiness is all that matters to me."

For a moment Wren didn't know what to say. She soon recovered, though, and asked, "Do you love her?"

He crossed his arms. "That's none of your business."

Wren couldn't take any more of this situation. She gave Anthony her most polite smile and rushed out of the front door. She didn't envy her mother for her complicated life, but a part of her did ask: *why does my mother get to be involved in a love triangle and I don't?*

She pulled out her cell and called her father's number. She didn't know where he was. He could be sleeping on a park bench for all she knew. *No,* she thought. *Dad's not that daft.*

"Hello?" her father answered.

"Where are you?" she asked desperately. "Are you okay?"

"I'm fine, though the park bench was a little uncomfortable."

Wren gasped, almost dropping the phone. "Why didn't you come to me for help? I have a spare room. I have three spare rooms!"

"The park bench is doing me fine," her father insisted. "The hobo that peed on me in the middle of the night was wearisome, but it did warm me up."

She hated it when her father made light of serious situations. He'd always done that, for as long as she could remember. Sometimes he was like a kid at heart.

"Dad, you will move in with me," she ordered him.

"You sound like your mother," said her father. "A bossy cow."

He hung up on her. She dialed his number again, and again, and again, but he blocked her.

"Damn both my parents," she whispered.

She knew she'd have to go and find her father in the park or she'd never be able to live with herself.

Chapter 7

Juniper smiled up at Fiona smugly from her desk and said, "And how's it going down there?"

"Fine," Fiona lied. "I'm doing well."

"Are you sure?" Juniper inquired coldly.

Fiona despised the angel in charge of her department. Juniper was a cold, unfeeling woman, faded from thousands of years of disappointments, enforcing the angelic laws with rigid strictness. Fiona hoped she didn't turn into her one day. That would be awful.

"I wouldn't lie to you," said Fiona sweetly. She could be very charming when she wanted to. "She's a bit of a challenge, sure, but I do love a challenge!"

"This one certainly is a challenge," Juniper muttered. Her silver eyes bore into Fiona with intensity. "I trust you haven't revealed to her your true identity? You know that isn't allowed."

Fiona was deeply offended by the insinuation and prepared to scream the place down with obscenities. She calmed herself quickly. It would be unbecoming to berate the boss in such a way, even if the woman deserved it.

"My lips are sealed," said Fiona.

Juniper grinned. "I like you, Fiona. I don't often single out any particular angel ,but you are an exception. I see potential in you. You could become one of the great guardian angels one day through hard work."

Fiona was speechless for a moment. She hadn't expected this. It was widely known that Juniper rarely took an interest in the angels under her, but when she did, that angel was meant for something great.

What's so special about me?

"Are you quite all right?" Juniper asked.

"I'm just surprised," Fiona admitted. Her hands were shaking a little. She had a lot to live up to now and it was terrifying. "I didn't know."

"Now you do," said Juniper. "So that means I expect more from you. Finish this assignment quickly and efficiently."

"I'll do you proud!"

Juniper sighed heavily. "I haven't been proud in a long time. I've forgotten what it feels like."

THE CELESTIAL CITY of Golden was home to over half a million angels. It was Heaven's next-door neighbor, with its own set of pearly gates. Every century or so the city planners would change the city's exterior to reflect their personal tastes. At the moment it was a cross between New York City and Venice, with high rise skyscrapers surrounded by canals and bridges.

Fiona was sitting on one of the bridges, watching the dolphins play in the canal below. She liked to watch the dolphins when she was depressed, which wasn't too often. She liked to think she was an optimistic, happy person all the time. What was it with this Wren woman that annoyed her and infuriated her so much?

Nobody has ever refused my services before.

Wren was her third charge. The previous two had gone smoothly. They'd wanted to change their lives and had accepted her help with grace. All she wanted to do was help put Wren's life in order. What was so wrong with that?

And I have to make Juniper proud of me.

Juniper may be thoroughly disliked, but if she saw something special in you then you worked like a horse to not disappoint her.

"What's up with you?" a voice asked.

Fiona's heart skipped a beat. That velvety voice could always send shivers down her spine.

"Hi Brock," said Fiona.

Brock had been in her class at angel training school. They'd been good friends since the first day they'd met, and she valued their friendship. She was also desperately and hopelessly in love with him. It could never go any further, though. Fiona didn't make friends easily, and she'd never act upon her feelings for fear of losing her friend.

"My latest charge is a bit obstinate," Fiona admitted, staring balefully into the clear canal waters. She tried not to look at Brock, with his wavy blonde hair, square jaw and strong shoulders. He was literally a sculpture of perfectness. "I've tried my best, but she just doesn't want my help. It's like she wants to be miserable and alone. I even tried to make her jealous, by claiming I was helping someone else called Damien, who wanted my help, but that didn't work either."

Brock sat on the edge of the bridge with her. He said, "I know what you mean. The world is cynical now."

"I'm a failure, Brock." She cried and felt him inch closer and put his strong arm around her. She could smell his musk and his wings tickle her neck.

"Have you given up?" he demanded.

Outraged, she said, "Of course not! I've never given up on anything in my entire life! Not giving up is the reason I died. If the prospect of German bombs falling on my head didn't make me give up, then an obstinate woman is not going to."

Fiona's memories of her death were still a little fuzzy, even seventy years after the event. She remembered jumping out of the back of the ambulance and going for the injured woman, who lay bleeding on that London street. She remembered the noise the Luftwaffe made as it glided overhead. She even remembered seeing half a teddy bear in the ruins of a house flash past her as she ran. After that, though, it was a blur. The only reason she knew a German bomb had blown her up was because her mentor angel had told her.

"Then stop crying and get back out there," Brock ordered her.

She wiped the tears away and said, "You always know what to say to me."

"That's what friends are for," he said.

She smiled warmly, though every time he called her "friend" her heart broke just a little bit more.

Chapter 8

The village of Snowflake Bay had the Atlantic on one side and trees on every other. They were literally in the middle of nature. Whenever someone in the village said they were "heading to the park" what they actually meant was the large fenced off area towards the west of the village. It was kept in perfect, prim condition by the SB Gardening Fanatics Society and often won awards. It was beautiful to spend time in, whatever the weather.

It's not beautiful if you have to sleep there.

Wren couldn't find her father anywhere. He wasn't sat at the bench by the frog pond, and he wasn't by the tables near the lemonade kiosk. She asked the kiosk's owner, Floyd, if he'd seen her father, but he just shrugged.

What was he thinking sleeping out in the rough like that in such cold weather? The old man could give himself hypothermia. Sometimes she despaired of her parents. The both of them were on a self-destructive streak that would eventually take the whole family down with them.

She eventually found her father by the bandstand, but he wasn't alone. There was a tall, heavyset man standing there with him. They were talking heatedly, her father looking quite intimidated.

What's going on?

The man reached forward. Wren panicked and ran forward, almost slipping in the wet grass.

"Do not touch him!" Wren screamed.

The man turned to Wren. His eyes were black and cold and his nose had been broken some time in the past. He looked like a bouncer.

"Get out of here," her father told her.

"Leave my father alone," Wren commanded, pulling out her cell. "Or I swear I'll call the police."

The man laughed and let her father go. He walked menacingly up to her and snatched the cell from her hands. She looked up at him, feeling like she was in the shade of a giant.

"Who are you?" he demanded, his eyes searching her.

Wren crossed her arms defiantly. "Who are *you*?"

The man grunted, smiled and said, "I'm Benedict Treadaway - someone Wick owes money to. But don't sweat it. It's all sorted now." His tone was half flirty, half threatening. "Or it will be, at any rate."

Wren couldn't help but frown. "Benedict Treadaway? That sounds like a posh actor in London's West End."

"You have a nice smile."

The man looked down at the screensaver of her cat on the cell before handing it back to her. He looked once more at her father before walking away.

Oh my God...my heart is beating like mad...

"You should never have interfered!" her father shouted. She'd never seen him so angry or so terrified before. "Do you know what kind of man that is? He's the kind of man what wouldn't think twice about putting a woman in hospital with serious injuries!"

She watched Benedict walking away. He stroked someone's dog as he passed them. He now seemed about as threatening as a budgie.

What a strange contradiction that man is.

"And what about you?" Wren demanded. "What are you doing involved with a man like that?"

"I borrowed money off him," he explained, looking down at his feet with shame. "I owe him a lot of money."

"All so you could lose spectacularly at cards."

He had a right to be ashamed. He'd involved himself and their family with some dodgy people and she wasn't sure she could ever forgive him for it. Benedict Treadaway may have flirted with her and stroked a passing dog, but there was no doubt in her mind the man was dangerous.

"I should just leave you out here and walk away," Wren stated. It was threatening to rain again. She really wanted to be indoors.

"You should do that," he said. "I don't want you involved."

She lifted his chin up to look at her. "But I'd never forgive myself if I let you freeze to death out here. You're coming to live with me and I'm not taking no for an answer."

Hope briefly flickered in his eyes, and Wren wanted to cry. He looked so wretched it broke her heart.

"I don't deserve any of you," Wick admitted.

She pulled him into a hug, figuring he deserved at least that. Besides, her father and the goon threatening him had both said the matter was sorted. Wren only hoped it was. She wasn't sure her heart could take another confrontation like that.

WREN SWITCHED ON THE TV as she heard her father splashing in the bath upstairs. She'd ordered him to wash as soon as they'd arrived home. He was starting to smell a bit. She'd splashed out on a giant bathtub while refurbishing the house. He'd have a whale of a time in it.

Gracie meowed and leaped onto her knee. She stroked her Russian Blue, feeling comfort from the soft fur of her companion. Soon Gracie's deep purr lulled Wren into blissful contentment.

"So, what are you and the other cats up to?" Wren asked playfully.

Gracie stared up at her with beautiful green eyes that spoke volumes. It said *I love you so much but this is my business.*

Wren smiled and tickled the cat's chin.

"Just don't get into trouble," Wren warned her. "I want at least one member of my family to be playing it safe."

"How did it go with your father?" Fiona demanded.

Wren ignored the angel, concentrating on stroking her cat. Fiona sat on the couch beside her, shuffling her backside to try and get comfortable. Gracie meowed at the intruder and allowed Fiona to stroke her head.

"You know Catherine the Great had Russian Blues?" said Fiona, tickling the cat under the chin. Gracie was loving every minute of it. "They're the royalty of the cat world."

"I know that," said Wren. "Why do you think I chose her?"

"She chose you. You went to bed one day and found her under your covers and she refused to leave." Fiona sighed. "I'm not going to go away you know. I hate to use the word stalk, but I'm going to stalk you until you let me help you."

"I don't have the strength to fight you."

If the angel was so hell-bent on sorting her life out, then she could do as she pleased. She pitied the person trying to arrange the mess that was the life of Wren King.

Fiona giggled with glee. "Excellent. We're going to have so much fun!"

"So, what is it you're going to do exactly?" Wren demanded, looking the angel in the eye. The woman's wings were conspicuously absent, and she was now wearing a tight pink top and a pair of jeans. She looked like a soccer mom out for a stroll.

"What do you mean?" Fiona asked.

"Are you going to just snap your fingers and magically make my life perfect?" Wren had meant to be sarcastic, but she suddenly perked up at the idea. "Wait, can you just snap your fingers and make my life perfect?"

"I'm not a wizard," said Fiona grumpily.

"But you made that cookie appear from nowhere yesterday, and you seem to be able to just appear and disappear whenever you want."

"I had that cookie in my pocket all the time. You just didn't see me take it out. As for the appearing and disappearing thing...that's the extent of my supernatural talents I'm afraid, and even then, doing that takes a lot out of me. I'm not exactly a higher-level angel you know. I can't just fly around the world." She seemed quite miffed about that. It seemed like a sore subject.

Wren said, "Can a higher angel snap their fingers and..."

"If all the higher angels and celestial beings snapped their fingers to make everyone's lives perfect then life would be pretty boring."

"It would be pretty darn wonderful, though."

"And it would be wrong. People have free will."

"Then what's the point of you?"

Fiona turned her face away, biting her lip. The woman looked like she was trying to control an outburst of anger. The diminutive angel had a temper that could crack a mountain in half. "I'm here to guide you," said Fiona through gritted teeth. "I'm not here to do everything for you."

Wren winced, realizing she'd hurt the angel's feelings. If she was going to be stuck with the woman for the foreseeable future, she didn't want any tension between them.

"I'm sorry," said Wren. "It's just I don't really understand any of this."

Fiona turned to her and smiled warmly. "It's okay. I know it's a lot to take in. I've just changed your whole universe."

"And my universe was pretty screwed up to begin with."

There was a sharp knock at the door. Fiona continued to stroke Gracie, ignoring it. Wren sighed, pushed the cat off her knee, and went to see who it was so early in the morning.

It was Jordan.

"Jordan, what are you..."

He thrust a pair of keys into her hands. Their skin met briefly, and she felt an electric thrill run through her body. "Dad wanted me to open up today, but I just can't be in the same room as him. Can you do it?"

"Why would you care about who opens the coffee shop?"

She really wanted to quiz him on what the argument was about but she didn't want to appear nosy.

"It's still a family business," he explained. His eyes looked puffy, like he'd been crying. He still looked pretty though. "I don't want to lose money. Please. You did good yesterday. I watched you. You're a natural."

"What about Aarna?" said Wren. "She's more than capable."

"She's quit. I don't know why. Just...please."

Wren blushed again, liking the fact that he'd watched her. It made her feel desirable, which didn't happen that often.

Unless you counted that gangster which threatened Dad, and... Cedric?

"Are you sure?" Wren asked.

Jordan sighed. "Perhaps later we could..." He pushed her against the door frame, kissing her, his hands clutching her sides like he didn't want to let her go. It lasted a mere five seconds before he grinned and left, leaving her shaken and on cloud nine.

She closed the door dreamily.

He really does like me.

As she flopped down on the couch, her skin tingling for what could be, Fiona cleared her throat.

"Why do you look like the cat that got the cream?" Fiona asked. She was excited, like she was on the verge of receiving some juicy gossip. Wren had the feeling the angel didn't have many friends.

She could hardly say the words. "Jordan kissed me."

"Greek God Jordan?"

"The one and only."

Fiona looked disappointed for a moment. "Oh. Seems like you don't need my help getting a man after all. I can still help you with..."

"He wants me to open the coffee shop. I think I've got a job."

Wren looked at Fiona's despondent face and felt a bit guilty. It seemed she didn't need a guardian angel after all.

"Looks like I'm not needed," said Fiona sadly.

I can't believe I'm going to do this.

"My life is far from picture perfect," Wren confided. "My parent's marriage is imploding and my father is being threatened by gangsters and I'm still not sure what I want to do with my life. I'm only opening the coffee shop up. It's not like I've got a full-time job. And Jordan? It's not as if we're getting married or anything. We're not even dating. Face it, Fiona, you have a long task ahead of you – a really, really, long and daunting task."

The truth made Wren feel miserable again, causing the euphoria of Jordan's spectacular kiss to fade away. She hated facing the truth head on, but sometimes it was the only way.

"You look sad again," said Fiona. "That's my fault. I'm sorry."

"Don't mention it," said Wren sulkily.

AFTER WREN HAD LEFT, Fiona found herself alone in the house. She felt a little awkward. This wasn't her home. These people didn't know her. She could hear Wick upstairs, singing in the bath. He was so out of tune she was surprised the walls didn't cave in.

She smiled. Her husband had been similarly tone deaf. Instead of annoying her it just made her love him all the more.

She pushed aside thoughts of the past and got up, deciding to have a snoop around while she had the chance. It was always a good idea to study the homes of charges. Sometimes a simple home makeover could improve someone's mood no end.

The walls were nice, a soft light brown. The furniture was wooden, expensive. The couch was fluffy and comfy and turquoise. It was a bit old, but not ready to be thrown out just yet. The house seemed far too spacious for just one woman. The poor dear must have been so lonely and bored all here on her own.

A framed portrait on the wall caught her attention. It was a family photo, taken perhaps five years ago. Wren's family wasn't large, but they seemed happy together. There was Wren, looking a little chubbier, smiling at the front. Stood next to her was her brother Leo, looking handsome in a tux and sporting a short beard. Dot and Wick were next, their smiles happy and content. Dot's two sisters, Annie and Anita, were there too, looking glum and miserable like two stone gargoyles. Sitting down in the middle like a proud patriarch was an elderly man, a triumphant and cheeky grin lighting up his features.

"Who are you?" a voice demanded.

Wick was standing in the doorway. He was wearing a pink robe, obviously one of his daughters as it didn't fit him very well. His hair, still black and thick as it always was, was stuck up all over the place.

He looks just like his grandfather.

Fiona smiled and announced, "I'm a friend of Wren. I just popped by to say hello but she had to rush off. She has a job at a coffee shop."

Wick smiled proudly. "Good for her. She's good at making tea and coffee. It's like she can make the perfect cup." He studied her intently before saying, "Do I know you?"

"You've probably seen me on TV," said Fiona.

Wick studied her for a moment. "Were you on American Idol?"

"Yes!" Fiona declared. "They even did this little segment on me but I didn't get very far. Simon Cowell said I sounded like a cat being strangled."

She hoped the lie was convincing. She'd never even watched American Idol, despite the fact it was streamed up into Golden. They could receive every TV channel on Earth up there. Flicking through every channel one by one literally took you all day. She was a fan of Indian soap operas. They made Spanish telenovelas look like Shakespeare.

"I better go and dress," said Wick, giving her a kind smile. He stared at her again for another second or so before saying, "I really think I know you."

"That's the power of TV!" Fiona declared.

She said goodbye and heaved a sigh of relief as he left.

That was close.

She gave one more quick examination of the room before flitting away. She appeared outside the Metropolis and sat down to wait for Wren to arrive.

Angels called their teleporting ability 'flitting." She quite liked the term. It sounded cute. As she was only a young angel she didn't have much magic in her, so she could only flit a few times a day.

I won't be a young angel for long.

WREN ROUNDED THE CORNER, still a little annoyed with Jordan for dumping such a responsibility onto her like this. She hadn't even had the chance to say no. Would she have said no? Maybe not, not with him kissing her like that. Or had he kissed her just to stop her saying no?

Was he using me, flirting with me, just so I'd cover his shifts at the Metropolis? She didn't think so. The argument he'd had with his father had turned violent. He probably didn't want to hurt Garrett again. *I wonder what the argument was about?*

It had to have been something deadly serious for it to conclude in face punching. She knew it was none of her business but she was dying to know.

Wren stopped when she saw Fiona sitting at one of the outside tables.

"How did you get here so fast?" Wren demanded.

"I teleported here...or flitted, as we like to call it," Fiona answered.

They were lucky the streets of Snowflake Avenue were deserted at this time of the morning. Anyone could've seen her just flitting in like that! Then again Fiona had flitted inside the coffee shop just the other day and nobody had noticed.

Wren looked at the glass doors of the Metropolis and noticed something odd. The door was only half closed.

"Have you been in already?" Wren asked.

Fiona looked confused. "How could I? You have the key."

"You could have flitted in and got one of the spare keys from inside the staff break room," said Wren.

"What are you accusing me of?"

Wren ignored her and pushed the door slowly open, senses alert for the presence of intruders. She wasn't scared; far from it. She ached to try out the self-defense techniques she'd learned so long ago on an actual petty criminal.

Fear me!

"Hello?" Wren called, finding the lights hadn't been switched off since the night before. Some of the tables hadn't been cleared either. The smell of coffee was strong and overpowering, even for a coffee shop.

"Come out," she shouted, hearing Fiona tip-toeing in behind her. The angel was wearing high heels and was making quite the racket on the tiled floor. "Come out now!"

She listened carefully, hearing a drip-drip sound. It was coming from behind the counter, near the coffee machine.

Wren gasped – the expensive coffee machine was gone.

"I think we've been robbed," said Wren slowly. She looked at Fiona, aghast. "Is this my fault? Should I have opened up sooner?"

"Don't blame yourself," Fiona assured her. "By the looks of it the break in happened last night."

"Snowflake Bay is virtually a crime-free zone; but then again Keegan did say there was a spate of burglaries in the area lately."

Fiona ignored her, her eyes searching the room for threats. The angel with the ability to teleport out of danger was more scared than she was.

"I better call Garrett," said Wren, heading to slip behind the counter. "He needs to know what..."

She put her hand to her mouth, stifling the scream that threatened to escape. She turned back to Fiona, her eyes wide open in horror, the gruesome sight she'd just seen etched forever on her irises.

"Wren?" Fiona asked, concerned. "What is it?"

Wren tried to pull together the words. "Someone pushed the coffee machine onto his head."

Fiona gasped.

"His head...it's split open like a watermelon," said Fiona, using the counter to prop herself up. She had a feeling she might faint. "Oh God..."

"Who?"

"Garrett. Garrett's dead."

Chapter 9

"**I** can't believe he's dead," Wren muttered, eyes closed. Keegan was holding her hand, the both of them facing away from the counter. She couldn't think about it.

"You should drink something with sugar in it," Keegan told her. He had a very soothing, consoling voice. "It might make you feel better."

"Are you sure it's Garrett? I just assumed it was him because he was wearing the clothes he wore yesterday."

She opened her eyes, determined to confront her fears. She wasn't going to shy away from this and let it ruin her life. She'd fought hard for the life she had now, and nothing would put her off.

"Was he murdered?" Wren asked.

"It's too early to tell," said Keegan. "But I'd be surprised if the coffee machine accidentally fell on his head. It looks really heavy."

Wren looked around, wondering where Fiona was. She'd probably flitted out of there as soon as the police turned up. She wasn't sure why she wanted the angel right now. Maybe because she'd been there when she'd found the body and could understand what she was going through?

"Come on," said Keegan. "I'll drive you home."

She looked up at him, wiping her eyes. "Who do you think did it?"

"I have no idea," Keegan admitted.

"Do you think there's a killer in the town?"

"You're starting to sound hysterical. This could still be an accident."

"You said it wasn't likely."

There was a commotion behind them. She turned around to see two white faced deputies, both of them desperately trying not to be sick, carrying away a black body bag. Sheriff Fisher watched them leave before turning to his son, his face grave. She'd never seen him look like this before.

This town has never seen a death like this before.

"I'll need you to come down to the station and make a statement," said the sheriff. "As soon as possible."

Wren nodded her head. "Is it Garrett?"

"We don't know," the sheriff admitted. His eyes were dark. He almost seemed to be on the verge of tears. "We're going to have to do tests, but we're fairly certain it is him."

She couldn't imagine the Metropolis without Garrett in it. While Wren didn't know him that well, she knew this place was his baby, his dream. It would probably be closed down now.

"Was there anyone with you?" the sheriff asked.

"I was with Fiona," she blurted out.

Damn! I forgot I wasn't supposed to mention her.

"Who's Fiona?" Keegan asked.

"My new friend," Wren answered.

What am I supposed to say?

"And where is this Fiona?" the sheriff asked. He seemed suspicious now, probably wondering why Fiona had left the scene of the crime.

"She was distressed by the sight of the body," said Wren, trying to sound sympathetic to her friend's plight. "She fled the coffee shop. I tried to stop her, but I knew I had to wait for you to arrive."

"I'll need her number."

Wren didn't think Fiona even had a cell phone. And even if she did, she didn't know the number anyway. Could you call up Heaven or wherever it was the angel lived?

"She doesn't have a cell," said Wren. "She thinks they give you brain tumors."

"Landline?" the sheriff asked. He was starting to sound impatient now.

Wren shrugged her shoulders. "I don't know it. Sorry. But she will be coming to my place later. I'll tell her then."

He didn't believe a single word she said, but he nodded his head and headed outside anyway.

He's going to think I'm hiding something. What if he thinks I killed Garrett?

"What are you playing at?" Keegan demanded, angry.

Wren smiled sweetly. "I have no idea what you're talking about."

"You just lied to my father," said Keegan. "Does this mystery woman have something to do with Garrett's death? Are you covering for her?"

"Of course not. Why would I do that?"

She had to get out of there before she put her foot in it even more. She was terrible at lying and she was only making things worse with every successive lie. Before she knew it, she'd be locked up in jail and arrested for murder.

"Why have you never mentioned this Fiona before?" Keegan asked. "I thought we told each other everything?"

"You've been busy lately," said Wren defensively. "I don't have many people to talk to."

Keegan crossed his arms. "That's no..."

"I need to go home," said Wren. "I'm still feeling a bit shaky."

"Wren..."

She rushed out of there as fast as she could. She hated lying to Keegan but she had no choice.

"What happened?" a voice called.

Wren stopped. Aarna was standing on the opposite side of the road in front of the closed down cat shelter. She wore a thick yellow parka and was ringing her hands anxiously.

"There's been a death," said Wren, crossing the road. "It might be Garrett."

"It might be?" Aarna asked. "What do you mean?"

So Wren told her everything she knew. Aarna broke down almost immediately.

"He can't be dead," Aarna wailed, crying. "He can't be dead!"

"It might not be him," said Wren. "We just don't know yet."

Aarna shook her head. "This is all my fault. This is...this is all my fault."

Wren was about to ask why when Aarna walked away. She tried to call her back but the girl didn't hear her.

What was that all about?

WREN CLOSED HER FRONT door behind her and leaned against it. She felt trapped. She'd made a terrible mistake mentioning Fiona and now she would have to continue to make up lies to keep her story in order.

I'm lying to the police! It's a criminal offence!

There was a note pinned to the wall near the black cat key rack. She picked it up and sighed heavily. It was from her father. *"Just popped out for a while. Don't worry about me."*

She did worry about him, constantly. He was more than likely either at the bookies or at another illegal card game. She thought he was sorting this out once and for all. At least that's what the big guy at the park said anyway.

Fiona peered up from the back of the sofa, her eyes full of concern.

"Are the police with you?" Fiona asked.

"I put my foot in it," said Wren. "The sheriff asked me if anyone was with me when I found the body and I said I was with you."

"Nobody is supposed to know I'm here! I'm your angel!"

"Well it's too late to change anything now. You need to make a statement and we need to come up with a story about who you are and where you're from."

Fiona stood up and crossed her arms. She pursed her lips, looking like an angry cat.

"Where I'm from is very complicated," said Fiona.

"We have to do something," Wren insisted.

"I should just go and leave you to it, but you'll get into trouble if I disappear now people know I exist. This is so vexing."

They made some coffee and sat down at the kitchen table. A radio played low-level rock music in the background and the cat was asleep on the floor, occasionally making odd noises in her sleep. She was probably dreaming about her next meeting of the local cat society.

Wren looked down at the notes they'd made. It had only taken them half an hour, but they'd put together a pretty decent backstory for Fiona. She only hoped it held up and the sheriff didn't look into it too much.

"So my name is Fiona McDonald," said the angel. "I'm your Facebook friend who you met on a page for Russian Blue fanatics. I live in Cape Cod. I married Angus McDonald when I was nineteen but he left me two weeks ago, only a few days after my beloved cat Chew Chew died."

"Why did he leave you?" Wren asked.

"He...God, this is so embarrassing. My husband would not leave me to become a monk! Let's say I'm a widower instead! That's more believable."

"We've decided. Stick to the story."

"I've moved here to be closer to the only friend I have left in the world." Fiona sighed in exasperation. "Even I know that you don't invite Facebook friends to live with you. I could've been an overweight Polish man for all you knew."

Fiona was right. They hadn't thought this through properly.

"So we talked on Skype a lot," said Wren. "We...we were proper friends, not just Facebook buddies. We sent each other Christmas and birthday presents."

"And... we went to online parties together. Wait, are they a thing? They sound rather lonely."

They laughed, coming up with an even more complicated back story to add to the one they'd already written down. It was fun. It was only when they'd finished that they both realized that they'd have to remember it all so they wouldn't get caught out in a lie.

"By the way, what is your real second name?" Wren asked. "Is Fiona even your real name?"

Fiona tapped her nose. "That would be telling."

The angel looked like a Fiona. The name suited her.

"Wait...does that mean I'm living here with you now?" Fiona asked.

"I suppose," said Wren. "I do have the room."

Why did I spend the compensation money on buying a house with so many rooms? It's just asking for trouble!

"Do you want to live with me?" Wren asked.

"I have my own apartment in Golden, but for the sake of the police and everyone else in town I'll be living here." Fiona smiled. "So, there we have it. My story is all sorted out. It's tragic and weird but it'll have to do."

Wren took a sip of her coffee, watching Fiona closely. She didn't seem like your typical angel. Then again, she hadn't thought angels were real until this pint-sized loudmouth turned up the other day.

"For some reason I expected angels to be tall and hunky," said Wren, feeling embarrassed.

"Some of them are," said Fiona dreamily.

Wren grinned, hoping to hear some juicy gossip. "Is there someone you've got your eye on? You can tell me anything you know."

"He's called Brock, and we've known each other a long time." She pulled at her hair and Wren slapped at her hand to make her stop. It was a habit her father had. It drove her crazy. "He's tall and muscular and has thick blonde hair and he's sort of my best friend and he has no idea that I like him."

"Tell him how you feel," Wren suggested.

Fiona shook her head. "What if I ruin our friendship? I don't have many friends, you know."

Wren smiled warmly. "You have one more now." Brock sounded like the perfect physical specimen. She couldn't wait to meet him.

"Anyway, I'm not here to talk about my love life," said Fiona, deftly changing the subject. "My job is to find you a boyfriend and a life."

"I doubt Jordan will have time for romance now," said Wren with a sigh. "Then again, romance wasn't what I had in mind with Jordan."

She smirked, her thoughts travelling to all sorts of naughty places. A romp in the sack with Jordan would have been so much fun and just what she needed right now.

"He was too young for you anyway," said Fiona.

"You're as young as the man you sleep with," Wren quipped.

Fiona laughed. "When was the last time you had a serious relationship?"

This wasn't a hard question for Wren to ponder. The answer made her feel like the most pathetic woman in the whole world.

"I have never been in a serious relationship," Wren admitted, her face going a deep red. "Not since Alex, and you probably know how that turned out."

"I do," said Fiona sadly. "But you mustn't let one disaster get in the way of you being happy."

Wren pondered this for a while but talk of Alex just made her feel more miserable than she already was. Besides, what right had they to talk of such trivial things when someone had smashed Garrett's head in with a coffee machine?

She noticed an envelope on the table.

"Dad must have brought the post in before he left," she said, opening the envelope. Inside was a card with a cute ginger cat on the front. It was from Cedric, the message reading, *"Loved our date. Hope we can try again some time."*

She couldn't help but laugh. She'd walked out on him and humiliated him and he still wanted more? Was he a glutton for punishment or did he truly have feelings for her?

"We only went on one date," she mused. "He can't have fallen for me. Even I know I'm not that adorable."

"Cedric lives in Snowflake Bay," said Fiona. "You've probably seen him hundreds of times over the years, right?"

"I guess, but we never talked or anything."

"Perhaps you should give him a second chance. He is a successful businessman, with his windows and doors business. You could be happy."

"He's about as interesting as a lemon." She thought it over for maybe half a second. "No, I did the right thing. Cedric is not the guy for me."

Garrett...

"I'm not sure I can think about dating right now," Wren admitted. "All I see in my head is Garrett."

"It was a trauma, though I've seen worse, especially..."

Fiona seemed to go quiet for a moment, and Wren suddenly had a revelation; to become an angel you had to die, right? How did Fiona die, or was it something you didn't talk about with angels?

"Anyway, I think I'm going to go for a nap," said Wren. "Today has been...long. Very long."

"We have statements to make to the police," Fiona reminded her.

"Are you my secretary as well as my angel?" Wren snapped. Fiona looked hurt for a moment. "Sorry."

"Maybe we both need a quick nap. I'll wake you in two hours."

Wren smiled. "Thanks."

FIONA FINISHED HER coffee as Wren went upstairs to bed. She wasn't sure what to do next. Her mission had seemed a simple one at first, but now it was twisting and turning in all sorts of odd and gruesome directions. She should really leave and then never come back, but that would put Wren in trouble.

"What do I do?" she whispered.

64

Chapter 10

"So, what do I do?" Fiona asked despondently.

Juniper regarded her icily before saying, "Are you seriously considering abandoning your charge to the fates?"

Juniper could read her like a book. That's exactly what she'd been contemplating. She'd never been involved with a murder before. She could handle German bombs but not something so calculated and evil.

"No, it's just that I wasn't sure how involved to get," Fiona explained. Her wings felt agitated. "I was just supposed to sort her life out and leave. That's how it always works. I knew this assignment would be different, knowing who Wren is, but I didn't expect there to be a horrible gruesome murder!"

"The murder was quite messy, I must admit. But you've seen worse. You saw a lot of things in London when you were a nurse during the Blitz. I didn't think a bit of gore would faze you."

"It did. It fazed me a lot."

She stood up, knocking her chair to the floor. This conversation was pointless. She already knew what she had to do. She could never abandon Wren now, not when she was so vulnerable. It would be tricky, trying to juggle all the lies, but it was only for a short while. Once Garrett's murder was solved, things would cool down and she could get down to the task of guiding Wren to the life she was meant to have.

What if Garrett's murder never gets solved?

Juniper sighed. "What's wrong now?"

"Nothing," Fiona lied. "I think I'm going to go back to my apartment and have a long think."

"Don't take too long," Juniper cautioned her. "You know what humans are like. Their lives can spiral fast."

On the wall behind Fiona was golden framed photographs of all Juniper's charges over the years. There weren't many. Juniper was very picky when it came to choosing angels. She wanted so badly to be one of those photos. She had to be a fully-fledged angel with all the powers that entailed.

WREN WAS WOKEN FROM a dream of exploding watermelons by her phone ringing. She sat up, her neck sore, and looked at the clock on the wall. She'd only been asleep an hour. Still, she felt rested, despite the nightmares.

It was Keegan.

"Don't you have a job to do?" she asked him. She stretched out on her bed. Gracie was sitting in the window nook, keeping watch on the neighborhood.

"I'm freaking out!" Keegan shouted. He lowered his voice an octave and cleared his throat. "This is a murder! An actual murder!"

"You must have known something like this might happen eventually, even in a small town like this."

"I don't know what to think. I..." He paused before adding, "I've found myself using skills I've never thought I'd get to use. I've helped look around the crime scene for clues and interviewed suspects. You need to come in and make a statement by the way." She grimaced as he continued. "I've even done some fingerprint analysis, though the results haven't yet come back from the state database. The technology we have at the local station is a little out of date."

She allowed him to rabbit on like this for another five minutes. He'd gone from freaking out to hyper enthusiastic in very quick time.

"Sorry for going on," he said. "Am I...am I sickened by this or excited? Am I a bad person if it's both?"

"You trained to be a police officer. You're finally getting to use some of that training. It's okay to be excited." *I think.*

He laughed nervously. "I suppose you're right. Anyway, I better get back to it. Dad's giving me the stink eye. Remember you and that mysterious woman need to make a statement. If you can't face it today, then tomorrow morning will be fine. Just don't leave it too long."

He hung up, not giving her a chance to spin more lies about
Fiona. Wren was happy for him. He really did love his job, and that
meant the killer would be found that much quicker.

What if Keegan is a rubbish detective?

She pushed that treacherous thought aside. Keegan was smart.
She had faith in him.

"I better get down to the station," she said to her cat. "Don't go
having any wild parties while I'm gone, will you?"

Gracie gave her a disgusted look, as if to say she'd never do such
a thing. Wren wasn't sure. Other cats had been in the house before
other than the ones she'd seen her pet with in the back garden. If
Gracie didn't want them in, she'd attack them, and she could be a
mean cat when got territorial.

WREN READ OVER HER statement for a third time, satisfied with
her version of events. There really wasn't much to say. She hadn't
seen much. She'd been too shell-shocked to notice any clues or
details around the crime scene.

"I still can't believe he died like that," Wren admitted.

The other deputies were sat at their desks, still as white as sheets.
Wren couldn't blame them. She still felt a little queasy herself.

"The coffee maker is quite heavy," Wren pondered, watching
with curiosity as the sheriff read over her statement. "How would a
normal person lift that up and use it as a weapon like that? They'd
have to have the strength of Dwayne Johnson."

The sheriff ignored her.

"I suppose you could push it," said Wren. "That might work. But
that means Garrett would have to stay still long enough on the floor
for someone to push it on him."

That seemed the most likely option. Was he knocked out first
and then murdered? Was he drugged?

"Are you sure it's Garrett?" said Wren. She waited impatiently
for the sheriff to finish. He was a very slow reader. "I mean I didn't
really get a look at his body other than to note he was wearing the
same clothes Garrett was wearing yesterday. Could it be the victim
isn't Garrett? It's not as if you can check his dental records or
anything. His skull was pretty much pulverized."

She saw one of the deputies rush off to the bathroom.

"I've known Garrett all my life," stated the sheriff, eyes not leaving his statement. Wren didn't think it was that enthralling. Why was he taking so long? "He has a tattoo of a moth on his right wrist. I was with him when he got it. It's him." He looked up at her, face serious. He'd been crying. "And I've had his DNA sent off for testing, just in case."

"I'm sorry," said Wren. "I know you were friends."

"I trusted that man with my life."

"Then you're the best person to look into this."

His words were grave. "And when I find out who did it, I'm not taking any prisoners."

Wren shivered a little. The look in the sheriff's eyes terrified her. He was a man to be reckoned with. She wouldn't like to get on his bad side.

"That will be all," said the sheriff.

As she was leaving she passed Fiona. She was talking animatedly to Keegan. They both burst out laughing.

"What's the joke?" Wren asked.

"I'd forgotten what a filthy mind Fiona had," said Keegan. His smile was as wide as she'd ever seen it. It was cute. "I've missed her."

Wren was confused. As far as she knew Keegan and Fiona had never met. Why was he acting like they were two long lost friends?

"We'll catch up later," Keegan told her, walking away.

Wren needed a moment to compose herself. It felt like she'd just slipped into another dimension. What was going on?

Fiona smiled sweetly and said, "He's such a good guy. You know he's the first queer person I've ever met? Wait, is it okay to say queer? They used to say that, and some other choice phrases, back in my time."

"I don't understand this," said Wren. "Why does he know you?"

"I'm not entirely sure. When I walked in he stared at me for what felt like an eternity and something seemed to come over him. He acted like we used to be friends but hadn't seen each other in a while. I just went along with it."

"Very strange indeed."

"Anyway, I'm here to make my statement. Wish me luck."

Wren left her to it, still confused about the whole thing.

A TEARY-EYED JORDAN was waiting for her outside her house. She considered walking away, pretending he didn't exist, but he looked vulnerable. She might be the only person he had to talk to seen as he was warring with his family.

"Can I come in?" he asked.

"Of course," she said. "Anything you need."

He grabbed her arms and pinned her against the ice-cold front door. It was forceful, but not violent. He looked into her eyes, into her soul, with a fierce passion. She gulped, her limbs trembling at the desire she saw in him.

The desire for me...

"I need to be with someone right now," he whispered.

"You're grieving," she said. "You don't want this."

He brought his mouth to her neck, tickling her skin with his soft lips. She melted almost immediately.

"WAKE UP!" A VOICE CALLED.

Wren pulled herself from her slumber. Her muscles ached and she was lying half off the bed, her head staring at the carpet. She was totally naked. She could see her underwear abandoned on the carpet. Her bras were almost ripped in half.

"What are you doing here?" Wren asked, pulling a sheet around herself. She couldn't keep the smirk off her face.

"I was waiting for Jordan to leave," said Fiona. "You've been at it all night. It's almost six o'clock the next morning!"

Wren smirked wickedly. "He left?"

"He snuck out of here like a guilty cat." Fiona crossed her arms. "I'm disappointed in you. How could you use him like that? His father was murdered yesterday! He's vulnerable!"

"He wanted me. Who was I to deny the wishes of a grieving man?"

Even to me those words make me sound like a douchebag.

"Let me get dressed," said Wren.

Fiona stormed out and slammed the door behind her.

WREN FOUND A SULKY Fiona sat at the kitchen table, twiddling with her hair, stroking Gracie. She refused to feel guilty. Maybe she had used Jordan, but he'd used her too. They'd needed each other.

"Why are you being so weird?" Wren asked.

"Nothing is going as I planned," Fiona admitted. "I didn't expect there to be a murder. This complicates things."

"I'm sure the police can handle it," said Wren. "Keegan studied criminology at community college."

Even then she had her doubts. She couldn't remember the last time they'd had a murder in Snowflake Bay. There'd been a hit and run once, and maybe an accidental death, but not a cold-blooded murder. What with the recent spate of burglaries the SBPD must be worked off their feet.

She sat down and poured herself a cup of coffee. She needed the caffeine. Being with Jordan made her crave the stuff for some reason.

"Are you and Jordan an item now?" Fiona asked.

"I have no idea," Wren answered.

"And what about your new job?"

"I assume I don't have one, not now the owner has no head."

Fiona speared her with an angry look. "That was crass."

Wren felt a little ashamed at herself for the joke. She was jubilant after her romp with Jordan. If she could get a young stud like him to go to bed with her then the world was at her fingertips.

"I'm being an idiot," said Wren.

"What do you mean?" Fiona asked.

"He just used me to smother his own grief," said Wren. "He's not into me at all. I could've been anybody."

"But he came to you. That's important."

She wasn't so sure about that. Perhaps the only reason he came to her was because she was the only one he could find at that moment in time. Still, a tiny, confident part of her screamed that he wanted her and only her. She only wished that part was the dominant one. She's learned the hard way not to be too optimistic.

"So, about the murder," Fiona announced. "I have a plan."

"Why would you have a plan about the murder?" Wren asked. She had a suddenly disquieting thought. "Wait, did you murder Garrett?"

"Of course not!" Fiona screamed, her tone appalled. "Why would you even ask such a thing?"

"Sorry, sorry."

Fiona was about to answer when they heard the front door slam shut. Wren tensed. She hadn't told her father yet about Fiona. What would he say? As far as he was concerned, she'd never mentioned a friend called Fiona before.

"Terrible weather," said Wick. "Thank goodness I have a warm bed to sleep in now!" He looked at Fiona and smiled again. "Good morning!"

"Morning, Wick," said Fiona.

Wren looked back and forth between the two of them. "When did you two meet?"

"Things happen when you're not around," said her father. He took his coat off and hung it on the old-fashioned coat rack near the back door. "I thought I'd go for a nice walk. Clear my head."

He smiled at them both and made a hasty exit.

"Was he acting shifty to you?" Wren asked, concerned.

"Why would he be acting shifty?" said Fiona. She was spreading some sort of black stuff onto her toast. It smelled awful. "He's just been out for a walk, that's all."

Wren picked up a small jar off the table. It was labelled "Marmite."

"What's this?" Wren asked. She stuck her finger in the jar and had a taste. She almost gagged. "It tastes like diapers!"

"I got a taste for it when I was stationed in London," Fiona explained.

"When were you in London?"

Fiona shrugged her shoulders and ate her toast. Wren sat down at the table, her mind going back to her father. Had he really been out for a walk?

"Dad's in debt to some loan shark," Wren explained. "He said he had it sorted though."

"Loan shark?" Fiona exclaimed. "This is serious!"

"I know."

"I know an angel in Heaven who was murdered by a loan shark! You can't be too careful with these people!"

Wren was about to demand an audience with her father when there was a knock on the front door. Her cat shot out from under the table, excited. She always became frisky whenever someone came. Gracie loved the attention.

It was Keegan.

"Morning," she said. "What's up?"

He looked forlorn as he said, "This isn't a social call, Wren. I'm here to arrest your father for murder."

Chapter 11

"Are you serious?" Wren demanded.

Keegan looked guilty as he said, "I'm not really supposed to say." He looked behind him, almost as if afraid of finding his father the sheriff hiding in the bushes. "Fingerprint analysis came back. Your father's fingerprints were found on both the coffee machine, the cash register, and the front door handle. We found his DNA scattered around as well. We think it's his sweat."

She couldn't believe what was going on. This had to be rubbish. Her father wasn't a murderer. He was a good man, despite his flaws.

"The results are wrong," Wren declared. "They have to be."

"They're not," said Keegan. "I'm sorry."

She stood aside, allowing him to come in. They could sort this out down at the station and her father could be declared innocent.

But what if he did do it?

Wren dismissed that thought. Her father had no reason to kill Garrett. As far as she knew, they barely knew each other.

"Are you just going to stand there all day or are you going to bring your father to me?" Keegan asked. He cleared his throat. "Sorry for being impatient."

"I'm sorry too," said Wren. "I'm just lost in thinking."

Her father had already heard the ruckus downstairs and come to investigate. He stood at the top of the stairs, his hands on the guard rail. He had a somewhat guilty look on his face.

"I know what this is about," said Wick.

As Keegan began to inform her father of his rights all Wren could think about was the ashamed look on Wick's face. Did he know he might get arrested? Why? Was it because he *had* killed Garrett?

Her father was led away, minus the handcuffs. At least Keegan had seen how difficult this was for her and had opted to make things a little easier.

"I heard it all," said Fiona, joining her by the open front door. "Do we need to go and get him a lawyer or something?"

"I'll phone my cousin Reba," said Wren. "She'll give us family rates."

She watched as her father sat in the back of the police car. Keegan gave her a slightly limp wave before he drove away.

"This can't be happening," said Wren frenziedly.

Fiona took her hand. "We'll get through this. I may not know your dad very well, but I know he's not a murderer."

"There's a lot of evidence that says otherwise."

THE TINY INTERVIEW room at the Snowflake Bay police station was beige. The furniture was old and rusting and there was damp on the walls. It was rarely used to interrogate suspects. Mostly the station cat, Shangela, slept in there. She was there now, curled up on the table, ignoring the awkward silence of the people sat around her.

"When are we going to start?" Wick asked.

"When your lawyer gets here," Keegan replied.

"I've already said I don't need a lawyer."

"I want to do this by the book."

Wick shrugged his shoulders and continued to stare at the two-way mirror on the side of the wall. He waved.

"Are you sure we're allowed in here?" Fiona asked, nervous.

Wren said, "Probably not, but Deputy Stark owes me a favor, and if he wants to spare himself the embarrassment, he'll do what he's told."

Deputy Stark gave her a filthy look before turning his eyes back to the mirror. He was their youngest deputy at only twenty-five. He sported a thick, muscular figure and a soft, brown beard. He was also terminally stupid. Wren owned a photo of him drunkenly taking a pee outside city hall the previous year.

"Is this the first murder you've ever investigated?" Fiona asked him.

"I didn't think there were murders in this town," the deputy admitted. He seemed quite devastated by the fact. So was Wren.

"My mom is scared witless. She wants me to go home and check her house is safe every night before I go home to my wife. It's not doing my marriage any good."

"I'm sure it's just a one off," Wren assured him.

Sheriff Rob Fisher was the next person to enter the interview room along with her cousin, Reba King. Reba always looked permanently harassed. Her lavender pant suit was creased and her ginger hair was tied back in a pony tail. She had a pile of papers in her arms which she flung haphazardly onto the table, disturbing the cat, who jumped onto Wick's lap. Cats always loved her father.

"Uncle Wick," said Reba, giving him a kiss on the cheek. "I've had such a busy morning. The twins have a cough and you know what toddlers are like when they think they're dying of some silly illness. How are you doing?"

"I'm being accused of murder," he stated.

She sighed and sat down next to him. She patted the cat briefly before turning to the sheriff and Keegan. Reba was all business now, as sharp as an eagle. She was known as *The Terror* in the courtroom.

"You can begin," Reba declared.

Wren grinned. Reba would get the truth out of her father and they'd be out of here in time for lunch. She just fancied a burger and fries.

"Warwick King, where were you between 11pm and 12pk the night before last?" Sheriff Fisher asked casually.

"No comment," said Wick.

"You had to have been somewhere. Surely you can remember?"

"No comment."

Reba sighed and whispered something in Wick's ear. He looked at her tersely and she nodded. He took a deep breath, as if ready to reveal something of major importance. Wren felt her heart skip. Was her dad really going to confess to murder? Did she really not know the man at all?

"No comment," Wick said again.

Reba said impatiently, "Now Uncle Wick..."

"This is my life we're talking about here," shouted Wick. "I'm sticking to this and you can't do anything about it."

"You're not going to tell me how your fingerprints and DNA got all over the inside of the coffee shop, on places where they shouldn't have been?" Keegan asked, talking for the first time since the interview started. "Maybe you touched them earlier in the day?"

"No comment," said Wick.

Wren couldn't take any more of this. She banged on the two-way mirror and shouted at her father to tell the truth, that he didn't do anything. This was only making him seem guiltier.

"Don't do that," said Deputy Stark.

"What's he doing?" said Wren. "He obviously didn't do this!"

"Then why not tell the truth?" said the deputy. "He definitely did it. He just doesn't want to implicate himself."

Wren felt like punching him. Her father was not guilty. She had to make him tell the truth, and so she banged on the two-way mirror again.

"Stop that!" shouted the deputy.

"Tell the truth!" Wren screamed. Everyone inside the interview room was looking at the mirror now. "Tell the truth!"

The mirror cracked, groaned like a coffin lid, and fell forward. It hit the hard concrete floor of the interview room, smashing instantly. Wren grinned sheepishly at the sheriff, who looked at her like she'd just burned down his house.

"Whoops," she said.

FIONA SMILED POLITELY, grabbed Wren's hand, and pulled her away. They needed to get out of there before anything else happened. She'd never been so embarrassed in all her life.

"No, no," Wren called, rushing back. "Dad! Dad! Why are you saying this? Tell them the truth! Tell them where you were that night!"

Wick turned away from her, pretending she didn't exist.

"Get them out of there Deputy Stark!" the sheriff cried. "Now!"

The deputy ushered them out of the side room, not accepting no for an answer. Wren tried to sneak past him but Stark was a big man. His arms were as thick as tree trunks.

"I have to talk to him!" Wren protested. "I can get him to tell the truth!"

"Leave him be," said Fiona. "He'll tell the truth when he's ready."

Wren gave her a treacherous look before storming away. Fiona considered following her but knew it wouldn't do any good. She needed time to let off some steam.

Why is Wick being like this? What is he hiding?

She stood by the interview room door, looking inside. Wick caught her eye for a moment. She saw shame and embarrassment written all over his face. He looked like a guilty man.

"No," she whispered. "No..."

THE BENCH OUTSIDE THE police station was brick hard but Wren ignored it. She had to sit down and think things through. Her thoughts were a mess. One half of her thought her father was guilty and the other didn't know what to think. If she'd watched this police interview on a cop show she would've assumed the perp was guilty. Why should the fact that the suspect was her father change anything?

"Your father killed my husband!"

Wren looked up to find a vengeful Katie standing in front of her. The woman looked like she was on the verge of starting a fight.

I can take her.

"My father didn't do this," Wren protested, standing up to face the woman. "He's...he's innocent."

Katie smirked. "You don't sound too sure about that."

The insolent, smarmy smile on the woman's face made Wren want to punch her.

"You know what? I actually did question my father's guilt back there. For a second, I thought he had to have done it, because why would he clam up? Now I know for sure he didn't do it. That man is not a murderer. He's hiding something but it's not that he pushed a coffee machine onto somebody's head. I trust my father completely." Wren hesitated before adding, "Well, not completely. He has his issues. But I know with every fiber of my being that he didn't kill Garrett."

"DNA evidence doesn't lie."

The vile woman was right about that. DNA evidence didn't lie, yet there had to be a reason her father's DNA was all over the coffee shop. Had he popped in to find her, or gone to see Garrett? Had he gone there to confront Jordan because he knew the man was sleeping with his daughter?

Katie pointed a finger towards Wren. "And stay away from my son. You're old enough to be his mother."

"What can I say?" said Wren. "He likes me."

Katie took a deep breath and said, "I'll see your psychopath father locked up for this."

"Your words have less poison in them than your Botox filled lips."

Wren crossed her legs and ignore the woman as she strode indignantly into the police station. She felt good. People like Katie got on her nerves. It was a pleasure to bring them tumbling down off their pedestal.

Perhaps Katie killed her husband? They do say the spouse is always the first to be suspected.

Fiona sat down beside her. "I have an idea."

"We have to prove my father is innocent," Wren declared.

"I know. Which is why we wait until Wick is put back in his cell and I flit us both in there so we can talk to him. Maybe he'll be so shocked he'll tell us the truth."

"Can you flit while with another person?"

"There's only one way to find out."

Fiona took her hands. They were shaking with terror. This did not fill Wren with confidence.

"Are we going to appear in a wall?" Wren asked dryly.

Fiona shrugged. "At least it will be a painless death. Probably."

Wren closed her eyes, waiting for something to happen. Would it hurt? Would her internal organs end up in the wrong place? Would she end up with three ears?

She tentatively opened an eye. They hadn't moved.

"Have you got stage fright?" Wren asked.

"I can't do it," Fiona admitted. She seemed on the verge of tears. "I thought I could do it but...I'm useless."

"If you think you can't do it then don't even attempt it. I want to live."

"I've failed you. You deserve a fully trained angel, not some trainee who can't even flit properly."

Wren pulled out a tissue from her pocket and handed it to Fiona, who was weeping openly now. The angel blew her nose loudly.

"Why do you think he wouldn't say anything?" Fiona asked. She tried to hand back her used tissue but Wren shook her head. "It was weird."

"He didn't murder Garrett, but he did do something," Wren admitted. "I've seen that shame filled look on him many a time, and it usually has something to do with gambling."

Fiona laughed. "Maybe he was gambling away his house at the time of the murder and was too ashamed to admit it."

The angel stopped laughing when Wren gave her a grave look. Had they hit the nail on the head? Had her father done something really, really stupid due to his gambling habit?

I need to find that man from the park. Maybe he knows something.

Chapter 12

It took Wren less than a minute to find Benedict Treadaway on Google. He owned a Western themed bar a mile or so out of town on the way to the city. She must have passed it hundreds of times while driving down the freeway. She could smell barbecue sauce and hear Dolly Parton serenading from a mile away. The place looked like fun.

"Are we ready for this?" Wren asked, nervous. "We're heading into the lion's den here."

"Surely he can't be that bad," Fiona insisted.

"This man is terrifying. He's a gangster of some sort. I wouldn't be surprised if we got shot the minute we walked in."

"You're very pessimistic."

Wren ignored her and headed for the door. She took a deep breath, put her hand on the handle, and pushed.

I should've worn a bullet proof vest.

The place was almost empty. A few men in their early thirties were lounging by the bar, drinking. A Dolly Parton lookalike was on a small stage near the back, lip-synching to *Nine to Five.* There was an abandoned Bucking Bronco with a giant pink cowboy hat on its head. It was all very normal.

"What can I do you for?" someone asked.

It was a man dressed as Reba McIntyre. He looked fabulous.

"Is this a drag bar?" Wren asked.

"You're not here to spout Bible verses and tell us we're going to hell, are you?" the drag queen asked. "If you are, let me sit down first. These heels are killing me."

Wren turned to Fiona, only to find her wandering off to listen to the Dolly impersonator. The angel seemed to be finding the whole concept of drag highly amusing. Wren had watched *Drag Race* for years and been to many drag shows with Keegan. She'd seen it all.

"You're Wick's daughter." The drag queen smiled and said, "I'm Bieber McIntyre, but you might know me as Benedict Treadaway. I own the The Good, the Bad, and the Fabulous."

Wren squinted her eyes, trying to find the imposing muscle man gangster under the dress, fake boobs, make-up and wig. He was there, but barely. She couldn't hide the fact of how astonished she was. He made a pretty good woman.

He looks better than me in a dress.

"You look good," Wren admitted.

Benedict bowed. "Thank you. I know."

Now that the pleasantries were over it was time for business.

"My father is in jail," said Wren. She tried to use her intimidating voice. "What did you make him do?"

"What do you mean?" Benedict asked. "What's happened to Wick?"

They sat down at a table by themselves. Benedict ordered them two glasses of water from a Shania Twain lookalike. He smiled and crossed his legs, revealing a pair of white lace panties.

He's tucked...

Wren explained about her father's incarceration and the murder of Garrett. Benedict seemed so completely shocked by this news he pulled his wig off.

"Wick isn't a murderer," said Benedict. "He's an idiotic gambler who won't take no for answer, but he isn't a murderer. Stupid man."

"So, you didn't have him murder Garrett to settle his debt?" Wren demanded.

This man didn't scare her, not when he was wearing lipstick and fake lashes.

"I run a secret card game out back every night," he admitted. "I'm not in the habit of having people killed."

"What happens when people can't afford to pay their debts?" Wren asked.

He fished inside the pocket on his dress and took out a cell phone. He placed it on the table.

"This phone has my accounts on it," he explained. "If someone can't pay what they owe I set up a payment scheme. People usually pay eventually. I may look tall and imposing, and I can act scary when I want, but I'm a pacifist. Usually just playing the role of a hard man is enough."

"Dad said he was going to pay you back."

"He obviously can't now."

"And you're not going to have him killed?"

The drinks arrived. Wren drank hers down in one gulp. She was still feeling a little nervous.

"Do you know how he was going to pay you back?" Wren asked.

Benedict shrugged. "Beats me, but..."

"But what?"

"You should talk to your mother about it. I only know what I've pieced together from the bits Wick has told me over the years. You probably wouldn't believe me anyway unless it came straight from the horse's mouth."

Wren was about to inquire further when Benedict, or Bieber McIntyre as she was known, walked away to serve another customer. Fiona was standing in front of the stage, smiling and clapping along to Dolly Parton. She was having the time of her life, oblivious to anything else.

What has my mother got to do with this?

"Drag is so much fun!" Fiona declared, rushing over to her like an excited schoolgirl. "We have to come back here again!"

"They have drag in Heaven?" Wren asked.

"Of *course* they have drag in Heaven! It would be Hell without it."

Wren was about to suggest they leave when her phone rang. She answered it without looking who the caller was. Big mistake.

"You finally answered!" declared Cedric. He sounded like the man who'd found a pot of gold at the end of the rainbow. "I'm so happy to hear from you. I've been thinking about you so much."

Do I have to put a restraining order out on you?

"I don't really have time for this," said Wren. "You know my dad's been arrested for murder?"

"I heard. The whole town is talking about it. I'm really sorry. I just thought you might want some help. My brother's a lawyer in New York. I know you'll probably go with Reba but Jackson is tough, and his firm could do this for you pro bono."

Wren was inclined to take up the offer. Jackson was one of the few success stories of Snowflake Bay. Everyone knew about the top law firm he was a partner in and the expensive condo he lived in. He was also known to be quite vicious in the courtroom. Would her father fare better if he had a shark like Jackson on his side? If it meant her father's freedom, then she'd let Reba go in a heartbeat.

"That would be kind of you if you could get Jackson in," said Wren, actually glad for Cedric's help. "It means a lot."

"We could discuss it further over a late lunch," Cedric suggested.

Ugh. I'd rather Dad go to jail. ...Free meal?

"Fine," said Wren, conceding defeat. She didn't feel like moving, and the barbecue in here smelled delicious. "Do you know where the 'The Good, the Bad, and the Fabulous' bar is?"

Cedric went quiet.

"Hello?" said Wren. "Are you still there?"

"Let's meet there tomorrow," Cedric answered quietly. "Same time tomorrow?"

"Fine," said Wren. "See you then."

Wren looked up to tell Fiona about the call only to find her angel gone. She was dancing on the stage with Dolly, wearing her own gigantic 1980s blonde wig that teetered precariously on her tiny head.

"Why am I surrounded by weirdos?" Wren muttered.

Chapter 13

It took all the courage Wren had in her body to knock on her
parents' door. She was scared she was going to find her mother's
naked lover answering again. She didn't think she'd ever be able to
scrub that sight from her mind.

Please don't be Anthony...

Dot opened the door. Her eyes were puffy were crying. She was
in her yellow dressing gown and her hair was tied back in a bun. She
looked like death warmed up.

"Oh Mum," said Wren, pulling her in for a hug.

It took a good ten minutes for Dot to calm down, plus another
hug and a cup of green tea. Wren had never seen her mother this
distressed before. It was a strange experience, seeing someone
who'd been so strong all your life act so different.

"Is this karma?" Dot wailed.

They were sat on the back porch on a swing bench. They had
their knees covered with a thick woolen blanket to keep out the Fall
chill. Dot and Wick's border collie, Ben, was running around the
garden chasing shadows.

"What do you mean?" Wren asked.

She wished Fiona hadn't gone back to the house. She might have
been able to tell her whether karma actually existed.

"Is my affair with Anthony causing all this trouble with Wick?"
her mom asked. "Is it karma for my indiscretions?"

Wren sighed. "And what about Dad's indiscretions? If anybody's
karma is to blame, then it's his. Not that I believe in any of that."

"I do love Wick so much. I just wish...I just wish he wouldn't put
his gambling ahead of us."

Dot leaned into Wren's shoulder, continuing to cry. Now was the
perfect time to ask her mother about what Benedict had hinted at.

"Do you know a man called Benedict Treadaway?" Wren asked.

"He owns a drag bar," said her mom. "I went there for a bachelorette party once."

"I don't mean Benedict Treadaway the drag queen. I mean Benedict Treadaway the illegal gambler and loan shark."

Dot took a deep breath. "Oh."

She stood up, letting the blanket fall to the floor. Dot looked away from her, as if trying to hide the emotions on her face.

"Dad also said he had a way to pay him back," Wren went on. "And then all of a sudden he's arrested for Garrett's murder."

"Your father is not a murderer," Dot insisted. She turned back to her daughter, her eyes wide. "But he was a highly renowned thief in his day. So was I." She grinned mischievously. "We were seventeen, childhood sweethearts. We skipped Snowflake Bay town to go and live in Boston because we wanted to be independent. It wasn't long until we got involved with this gang and pretty soon we were running the show. Nothing petty like simple burglary, but high-end stuff. We stole from the rich and gave to ourselves. It was such a turn on." She smiled again. "Those were magical days. Then we got too ahead of ourselves and tried to rob a gold exchange. We got caught almost straight away and sentenced to twenty years in prison."

"You went to jail?"

"We both got parole after ten years and got married the day we were released. You were conceived that very night. The day after we moved back to Snowflake Bay to be near the rest of the family. We've been happy-ish ever since."

This was the most convoluted story that Wren had ever heard, and yet it made sense. Her parents were thieves.

"Are you shocked?" Dot asked. "I'd be shocked."

"I'm very shocked," Wren admitted. "And I'll process it all with a tub of ice cream later. But I don't see what this has to do with Dad and Benedict Treadaway."

"This is only a guess, but..."

It all slotted together like the pieces of a puzzle. Wren knew what was going on, or at least part of it. The realization didn't make her feel any better. Far from it.

"Dad is behind the spate of burglaries in Snowflake Bay," said Wren. "He's turned back to his old life of crime to pay back Benedict."

Dot said, "I suspect so, though I don't know for sure."

"That's why his fingerprints and DNA are all over the coffee shop, especially the cash register. He was robbing the place. He must've come across Garrett, thinking the place was empty, and then he..." Wren shook her head. "No. Dad didn't kill him. He'd never resort to murder, not even if he was desperate to cover up his tracks."

She didn't like the fact that her father was robbing from his own town, but it was better than murder. Just.

"Does Dad have his own desk or drawer or special place in the house?" Wren asked. "Maybe we can find something to confirm whether he really has gone back to his old ways."

"He loves to sit in his garden shed and watch football," said Dot. She smiled. "He was always so happy whenever he got to spend time alone. It made him very horny."

Wren grimaced. "I don't want to know."

The shed was large, made from sturdy wood. Inside was a ratty old couch and a 50-inch flat screen TV. There was gardening equipment hooked onto one of the walls. They looked unused.

Where would he hide something?

There were several drawers. Inside she found old copies of TV Guide and ancient betting slips. On the shelves were just old tins of paint, bottles of turpentine and her father's cooking trophies from the local bake-offs they had at the town hall. The man loved baking.

"I can't find a thing," said Dot. She sat down on the sofa. "This is quite comfy. No wonder he likes it in here."

Wren walked across to join her mother, hearing the boards creak under her. Suspicious, she kneeled down on the floor.

Wren said, "This would be a cliché, but they are clichés for a reason."

She quickly grabbed a screwdriver from the rack on the wall. She managed to pry open the wooden board with ease.

Too easy, almost as if it had been opened recently.

"Bingo," Wren declared.

They pulled out everything from under the floorboard and placed it in a pile on the couch. It was damning evidence of her father's recent foray back into burglary – lock picking kit; black balaclava; bundles of money; bags of gold and silver jewelry. There was even a pack of Lotto scratch cards.

It took them a while to count the money. There was at least fifty grand, all in various used notes.

"We can pay off Benedict with this," said Wren.

"It's stolen money," Dot insisted crossly. "It's not right."

"You really don't have the high ground here."

"Your father stole from local businesses, from friends, from people we see every day when we walk about town. I'm not sure I could look any of them in the face ever again if we didn't find some way to return this money."

She knew her mom was right. Doing the right thing was better than profiting from a crime. Besides, she trusted Benedict not to murder her father for not paying him. He seemed genuine. She wasn't quite sure why but she trusted him. Maybe it was the high heels?

"Let me handle this," said Wren.

Chapter 14

"What's taking them so long?"

Wren and Dot were hiding behind a large bush in the park. They'd placed an anonymous call to the police and told them they'd leave the stolen money and merchandise underneath the bench nearest the bandstand. The police had yet to turn up, and it had been an hour. She was pretty sure if the police didn't claim it then someone else would. Wren would wrestle whoever tried to grab the bag to the ground if need be.

"Perhaps they're busy," Dot suggested.

"This murder really threw them," said Wren. "Maybe you're right."

"They're not used to dealing with anything more serious than a missing rabbit."

"Keegan has a sharp mind. I know he can do this."

Someone tapped on Wren's shoulder.

"I thought I recognized your voice," said Keegan. It sounded like a reprimand. "You should've downloaded one of those voice changing apps."

Wren blushed. "Keegan..."

"Let's sit down and you can tell me everything."

Dot shrugged. The game was up.

JUNIPER STUDIED THE living room with distaste and shook her head.

"I don't like it," the head angel admitted. "Wren has very poor taste."

Fiona crossed her arms, trying not to scowl or show she was annoyed. When she'd received the telepathic summons from Juniper, she became very frustrated. The murder case was starting to get interesting and she hated to miss out on anything. Besides, it was way more fun than being an angel life coach.

Did I really think that?

"What brings you to visit?" Fiona asked. "I'm kind of busy."

"I had work to do on Earth and decided to pop in and see how you're doing." Juniper wiped her finger across the tip of a shelf. It came away caked in dust. "You seemed to be in quite the sorts when you last visited."

"I got over it," said Fiona. "You know what I'm like! I worried over nothing."

Juniper gave her a look that spoke volumes. Fiona cleared her throat and hurried into the kitchen, her boss following. She started to fill the kettle.

"Tea?" Fiona asked.

"Would you like to be transferred to another case?" Juniper inquired. "Is that why you're acting so odd?"

"No." She sighed heavily. "It's not that."

"I may have a reputation as a fearsome angel, but I do care. Speak to me."

Fiona leaned against the kitchen counter as the kettle boiled.

"I found myself enjoying things down here too much," Fiona admitted. She lingered a little. "And then I realized that it could be over at any time. As soon as Wren sorts her life out I'll be sent back to Heaven."

Juniper nodded. "You don't want to leave her."

"It's not just her. It's everything here, in this town. She has a family and friends and a place to live that's special. I had none of that." She sighed again. "I was brought up in Atlanta by a rubbish dad and escaped by marrying the first man who took an interest in me. I thought things would change, but Richie was always working, and deep down I'm not sure he ever loved me. So, I tried nursing. That was where I felt I came into my own! I loved helping people. It gave me a purpose. And then when I fell pregnant..."

"Raking up the past is bad for an angel. It does you no good. I was burned to death as a witch. If I kept thinking about that time, I'd end up insane, and you know what happens to insane angels."

Fiona gulped. She did know what happened to insane angels. They became demons.

"So, I should just get on with my job, not think of the past, and be a good girl?" Fiona asked.

"Nobody's saying you have to stop enjoying your job, but you have to slightly detach yourself from it. I know it's hard, especially considering who Wren is, but it's the best thing to do."

The kettle started to whistle just as Juniper flitted away. Fiona realized the angel was absolutely right. She had to be professional about this. It was just a job, nothing more. If she'd become attached to every patient she'd had when she was a nurse it would've driven her mad. Wren was just another client.

But she's not, is she?

KEEGAN NODDED, TAKING it all in without protest. He didn't interrupt. He didn't make any disappointed faces. He just listened.

"I could arrest you for this," he told them.

"You already know you won't," Dot insisted. "Otherwise we'd be in handcuffs right about now."

"Don't tempt me," said Keegan.

Wren felt like everyone passing by was watching them, looking for the bag of money and stolen items. It reminded her of the time she was in the school Nativity play and had forgotten her lines.

"Why are you being so kind?" Wren asked.

"You need to put this stuff back under the shed and wait for your father to confess," Keegan explained. "Otherwise he may go down for murder."

"Except he'll go down for burglary instead, and with his criminal record he could go down for a long time!" Dot railed, angry. "I will not let that happen!"

"He could die of old age in prison if he gets life for murder," Keegan reminded them. "Would you prefer *that*?"

Wren could see her mother's rage boiling over, and Keegan's understanding and patience being sorely tested. She knew she had to be the middle ground here. She could sort this.

"We'll put the money and the valuables back under the shed," said Wren. She could see the sense in it, but it still felt like a failed plan. "But let me talk to my dad. I can convince him to tell the truth."

"I suppose I could allow that," Keegan conceded.

"Hmm," Dot grunted. She eyed Keegan suspiciously. "I've never trusted a cop."

Wren slapped her mother's hand. She was being rude.

"Do you truly believe Dad didn't do this?" Wren asked him. "I want to know you believe him."

"I know your father really well. He was my mentor when I was kid and I joined the Snowflake Bay Amateur Dramatics Society. He's not a killer."

Something passed over Keegan's face. Wren was sure he was keeping something hidden from them.

"Mom, go home," said Wren. "Keegan and I can take care of this."

Dot nodded. "I think I need a nap anyway. All this is really making me tired." Her mother walked away, leaving the two of them alone.

"You already knew about my parents and their pasts," Wren stated.

Keegan grinned. "I can't keep anything hidden from you. Yeah, I already knew. Wick told me when I was fifteen. I was confused about who I was, and he offered up a secret to try and make me open up."

"Dad knew you were gay all the way back then?"

"He was the only person I had to confide in."

Wren had always known her father and Keegan were close, but this was something different. Wick had been Keegan's confidante for nearly twenty years.

Dad knew Keegan was gay when I went on that date with him.

"I found Wick's stash when I was searching his property," Keegan admitted. "I stopped the other deputies from searching in the shed. I couldn't let them find it. Now I realize how stupid that was. If they'd found it Wick would've had to confess to the burglary and he wouldn't be up for murder."

"He was at the scene of the crime. The police would only have his word that he didn't kill Garrett."

"I know that."

Wren managed a smile and leaned into Keegan's shoulder.

"This is a right mess," she admitted. It was so convoluted she almost smiled. "Whatever we do, Dad will end up in prison, and we can't prove he didn't kill Garrett."

"Then we prove it," said Keegan. "*I* prove it."

They talked a little more about how hopeless it was. There were no CCTV cameras in the shop. Wick's fingerprints were the only ones on the murder weapon, the coffee machine. Nobody had seen anybody else leave or enter the premises as Garrett's time of death was late at night.

"Wait," said Wren. She was appalled nobody had even considered this. "Dad's fingerprints were the only fingerprints on the coffee machine?"

"Yes," Keegan answered. "That's right."

"That doesn't make sense. I touched that machine. So did Jordan, Garrett and Aarna."

"That machine gets dirty every single day. Garrett most likely cleaned it before he was murdered."

Wren groaned. He was right. Then again, the real murderer could've cleaned it to cover up their own tracks. There was no way to be sure. They needed rock hard proof to prove her father's innocence.

"I'm only at the beginning of this," she admitted. "I can't expect to solve it straight away."

"You're planning on solving this?" Keegan asked, raising his eyebrows.

"Maybe."

She'd watched TV shows and read books about amateur sleuths before. The local police never took the interference of meddling spinsters very lightly. Wren and Keegan may have been close friends, perhaps best friends, but she didn't want to ruin things by causing him aggravation.

But if meant clearing my father of murder I'd annoy the hell out of him, friend or no friend. Family comes first.

"Let's go talk to my dad," she decided. "We might be able to clear up some of this mess."

THE SHERIFF PROTESTED, but in the end, he saw the wisdom in allowing Wren to talk some sense into her father. Thankfully he didn't believe Wick was a killer either, but he had to go with the little evidence he had. Wren was pretty sure if things didn't turn out as planned the sheriff would lock him up.

The police station was small, so they only had one cell. It was clean, with metal bars and a proper single bed. The walls were white and had obviously just been recently painted. Wick was sitting on the edge of the bed, looking dejected and pathetic.

"It's just you and me now," said Wren.

Wick looked up at her. "No comment."

"Between my own investigation, and through talking with Benedict, Mom and Keegan, I know pretty much everything." She tried to hide a smirk. "Did you and Mom have your own criminal nicknames?"

"The local press dubbed us Little and Large." He laughed. It made Wren's day. "It was quite rare you'd see a married couple who were burglars and robbers where the wife was much taller than the husband."

She sat down beside her father on the bed. It was quite comfortable.

"You know you have to tell the truth," she said. "It's the only way to clear your name."

"If I go down now, then this is it. I'll die in prison."

"You just robbed a few shops. You might get ten years."

He looked her in the eye. He was frightened.

"Your mother didn't tell you about my first stint in prison, did she?" Wren shook her head as he continued. "I was sixteen. I punched Sheriff Fisher when he caught me shoplifting. I served six months in an adult prison. He thought it might scare me straight if I saw how bad those places were. This will be my third strike. Wrenny, I'm knocking on seventy. If I go to prison now for any crime, I probably won't live until my release date."

Wren didn't know what to say. Her father was going to die in prison whatever he was charged with.

He doesn't look old, does he?

He was short, and a little bit overweight. There were deep lines around his eyes and it was clear he looked his age. He was an old man. Her father had aged before her eyes and she'd only ever saw the young man she'd known as a child.

She pulled him into a hug. He smelled of the cheap soap he used. It was a familiar fragrance that brought to mind memories of childhood; him pushing her on the swings; buying her ice creams;

taking her to look at the cats in the shelter. Her father was precious to her. She couldn't live without him.

"What do we do?" Wren pleaded.

"It's the principle of the thing," Wick insisted. He wiped a tear away from Wren's cheek. "I will never admit to murder, because I didn't do it, but I'll admit to the robberies."

"We gave the money and stuff back to Keegan," Wren said. "He's going to give it back to all your victims." She hated the word. "Sorry. Victim sounds too harsh."

"Harsh, but true. I shouldn't have done it. I ruined everything. I just got so desperate that..."

He turned away. Wren clutched his hand as he started to weep.

He went on. "I knew deep down that Benedict wouldn't hurt me, but the gambling got in my head. It made me panic. I had to do something to sort it out."

"It's okay," said Wren.

He turned back to her. His face was resolute, brave.

"Tell the sheriff I have a confession to make," he said.

"I KNEW WHAT TIME GARRETT left every night. He locked up at 10pm exactly. I knew because I'd watched him do it for a week. He'd go over the place, cleaning everything from top to bottom. No wonder he had a five-star cleanliness rating."

"Garrett always kept a clean ship," said the sheriff. He smiled contemplatively. "When we were at school he always had the tidiest locker."

Wren was sitting on a chair next to her father in the interrogation room. Reba was sat on his other side, nodding and writing things down as her father explained what happened that night. She hadn't been pleased when they'd told her that he was going to make a confession, but her father had talked her into it. Shangela the cat was in her usual place on the table, keeping a careful watch on proceedings. The brown tabby took everything in, almost as if she understood it.

"That means the murderer *did* clean their own fingerprints off the coffee machine!" Wren declared. The sheriff glared daggers at her. "Sorry. Just thought I'd mention it."

The sheriff nodded. "We'd already considered that."

"Please continue," Keegan asked.

Wick looked down at his hands. His nails were bitten raw.

"It was about a quarter to midnight when I arrived. I didn't see anyone leave the Metropolis, but the front door was wide open. The lights were off, but you could still see around inside because of the moonlight reflecting off all the silver and chrome fixtures. It was actually quite pretty." Wick took a sip from a glass of water and cleared his throat. "I went inside but nothing was amiss at first. I figured that maybe he'd just forgotten to lock up. I went to the cash register and opened it. There was about a grand inside, which I put in a bag. That was when I noticed that the coffee machine was missing." Wick looked away. He was getting to the gruesome part of his tale. "I walked forward, almost tripping over Garrett's feet. He was on the floor. The coffee machine had somehow toppled over and..." Wick went pale. He took another sip of water. "It must have hit his head and..."

"Killed him," the sheriff finished.

Wick nodded. "I didn't know what to do. I tried to push the coffee machine away but it was heavy, and so I ran."

"You should've called me."

"I didn't want you to think I'd killed him."

The conversation continued, her father admitting to all the stores and businesses he'd robbed, some in Snowflake Bay, and several in the city. Some of them happened before he'd gotten into debt with Benedict, which meant that hadn't been the factor that had forced him back into crime. Wren stared daggers at him when she found that out.

"I know what you're thinking," said Wick.

Wren was calm as she said, "I'm thinking went back to crime because you enjoy it, not because you were in debt."

"It was a little of both."

Wren waited while her father signed his confession. It all seemed so straightforward, but he was still signing his life away.

"Will this confession help his case?" Wren asked.

"Probably not," said Reba. She patted Wick on the arm. "But I'll fight to keep him out of jail."

"Just a few more questions now you're being forthcoming," said the sheriff. "Did you notice anything else out of the ordinary?

Garrett doesn't usually stop at work late. He's always been punctual."

"There was nothing," Wick admitted. He looked thoughtful for a moment. "No, wait, I did hear something. I'm not sure. There was a noise in the back room. I think that's where the staff has their bathroom and kitchen?"

"That's right, though it's like a little corridor that leads off to a few tiny rooms," added Wren, trying to feel useful. "There's also the public bathroom, and a small office where Garrett does his paperwork."

"What kind of noise?" Keegan asked.

Wick shrugged. "I don't know. Just...sort of a squeaking, creaking noise. I thought it might be a bird at first, an owl or something, but now I'm not so sure. Maybe it was the murderer."

Wren felt terrified. Her father had been in the same store as a cold-blooded murderer. If he'd entered the premises just a minute or so earlier then he could've been killed too to cover up the crime.

"That's it," said Wick. "That's everything."

The sheriff nodded. "Thank you for finally being honest. I appreciate it."

"What does this mean? Can I go home?"

It was getting late. It was already dark outside. Wren was tired and hungry, and she was curious about where Fiona had been all day. The angel had just seemed to have disappeared.

"I'm sorry," said the sheriff. "Normally I would, but I can't take the risk that you'll flee the county. I really am sorry."

"Sheriff, my father wouldn't do that!" Wren protested.

He probably would.

"It's okay," said Wick. He laughed. "I was thinking about making a run for it, but I wouldn't have gone through with it. I couldn't leave my family."

Wren smiled sadly. "Oh, Dad."

"I FINALLY WORKED UP the courage to see you," Fiona whispered.

The graveyard was quiet as the sun went down. Fiona was all alone. For hours she'd walked back and forth outside the fence, scared to go in. She knew the moment she saw the grave she'd break.

"I'll bring you some flowers the next time I pop by," she said, noticing the gravesite was overgrown with weeds. "When was the last time someone came to see you? This is not on."

She started plucking out all the weeds, trying to calm her temper. He didn't deserve this.

WREN SAT DOWN ON THE bench outside the station, feeling mentally exhausted. Today had been a very long day. Tomorrow would be even longer. She had a lot to do if she was going to find out who killed Garrett.

I've done good so far, right?

Delving into her father's past and getting him to admit to the burglaries were probably the easy part. He was a man she knew, or thought she knew. Now she would have to investigate strangers, or at least people she knew only slightly. Would they even talk to her? Would they be hostile, or lie? What would she do if she did find out who the killer was?

"How did everything go?" Fiona asked.

Wren almost jumped out of her skin. She hated it when Fiona did that.

"Where have you been all day?" Wren asked. She knew she was taking out her frustration on the angel but at the moment she didn't care. "Some angel you are."

"My boss came by for a spot inspection," Fiona explained. She sounded angry. "But I worked through it."

"That took you all day?"

"She's a very hard woman to please."

That she was lying, or embellishing the truth, was not lost on Wren. Fiona couldn't lie for toffee. She decided to leave it, though. The angel deserved some privacy. If she wanted to tell the truth she would, in her own time.

They headed back home, which wasn't far. Wren explained what had happened during the day as they walked. The night air was crisp, not too cold, not too hot, the perfect Autumnal weather. Wren's favorite season was Winter, but she did love the Fall. Or was that pumpkin pies she loved?

"Sneaky old bugger," Fiona muttered.

"At least he's not a murderer," said Wren. "It's not much comfort. He's going to jail either way, but at least he's not a murderer."

"We'll find a way out of this."

She wasn't sure there was a way out of this. The only thing that could get her father acquitted was either a miracle or a sleazy lawyer.

Cedric's brother...

"Cedric told me his brother had offered his services," said Wren as they came upon her garden gate. "I think he could get father off, say his mental faculties were impaired because of his gambling addiction or..."

Fiona stopped in front of her. Something was wrong.

"What is it?" Wren asked.

The words 'Don't Be Nosy' were spray painted on her front door.

Chapter 15

Sleep failed to come for Wren that night. All she could think about was the message on her front door. Was it a threat, or did it have nothing to do with Garrett's murder? Who knew she was investigating it apart from the police and her family? Was someone watching her?

She sat up in bed, feeling Gracie's curled up bundle under the sheets. She was like a hot water bottle. Normally the feel of her cat's silky, warm fur was enough to drown out any anxieties, but this was different. Nobody had ever threatened her before.

Wren pulled out her laptop and watched some crazy cat videos for an hour or two. Sleep still wouldn't come. She did some star jumps, almost falling over her Persian rug. Sleep still wouldn't come. She decided there was only one thing for it – she would have to start right now on the murder.

What do I do first?

She needed to make a list of all the possible murderers and their motives.

"I need a pen," she muttered, switching the light on. The clock said it was almost five am. "Pen..."

She started rummaging around in some drawers. She found old cinema stubs, a failed attempt at crocheting a hat for Gracie, and her wedding photo, still in its gleaming golden frame.

"I look so happy," she muttered sadly.

Alex looked so dashing and handsome in his tuxedo. His smile was even wider than her own. Had there ever been a couple as happy as they were on that day? Had there ever been a couple as miserable as they were on the day they decided to call it quits? She still missed him.

"I'm sure we could've worked it out," she whispered.

They'd tried to make things work, but the trust had gone on both sides. What was the point in staying married when neither partner trusted or had confidence in the other?

She went through the next drawer down and grabbed a cheap notebook and a pen with a pink fuzzy haired troll stuck on the end. She grinned and went back to her bed, eager to begin.

The first person on her list had to be Jordan Knowles. As much as it pained her to admit it, he had more than enough of a reason to kill his father. They'd had a serious argument that had led to an assault. What was the argument about?

Katie Knowles. Garrett's wife was a vile woman who had also argued with her husband the day of his death. Was the argument about Jordan's beef with him, or was it something entirely different?

Aarna (she didn't know her second name). The barista worked at the Metropolis, and so knew Garrett, so she had to be added to the list. Plus, she'd seemed very, very upset over her employer's death – perhaps too upset? She'd also quit the day of his death, and she seemed to think it was her fault Garrett was dead.

Wren couldn't think of anyone else. The only other person she knew that Garrett had a personal relationship with was the sheriff, and he wouldn't murder anyone. He was the law giver, not the law breaker.

Would he?

She hesitantly added Sheriff Fisher to the list. He'd known Garrett all his life. They were best friends. He probably knew secrets even Garrett's wife didn't know. Was he the cause of the argument between Garrett and his son?

Veronica Van Clark. She'd opened up a coffee shop down the street that was doing badly. She'd even tried poaching some of Garrett's customers while Wren was there. Could she have killed Garrett in revenge? Would she do something so brutal over such a petty thing?

Before she knew it, the sun was up. She opened her curtains and looked out across the street. The big house with the huge oak tree out back had a for sale sign stuck in the middle of its front garden. She hadn't noticed it before. Still, it was time. Mrs. Rison had moved to a retirement community after her husband died and her kids had been begging her to sell it ever since.

Wren missed Mrs. Rison. She would pop over occasionally with a batch of her signature M & M cookies and they'd chat. She still managed to pop over to see her at the retirement community from time to time but it wasn't the same.

She heard a meow and looked down to pat Gracie. It wasn't Gracie. It was the black cat she'd seen her little one playing with the other day under the gazebo.

"What the heck are you doing in my bed?" Wren shrieked. The cat ignored her. "Hello? Are you listening to me?"

Gracie was curled up next to the black cat and they were grooming each other. It was utterly adorable. Her anger fizzled away.

"I guess I have two cats now," Wren mumbled.

Something was familiar about the black cat. She'd never gotten a good look at it before but she could swear it was Mrs. Rison's cat, Casper. Wren thought she'd taken her feline friend with her when she'd moved. Had it run away to come back to the only home it knew, or was it just a coincidence?

She stroked the newcomer and tried to find its collar under the mounds of silky black fur. Wren had never seen fur so thick, and the cat itself was enormous. It was probably a Maine Coon.

"Hmm," she said, locating the collar. It was rainbow striped. "You're definitely Casper. I better phone Mrs. Rison and tell her."

Both cats were now fast asleep. Wren shoved the notepad under her pillow, gave both of her furry friends a pat on the head, and climbed back in bed. She fell asleep almost instantly.

"ARE YOU SURE?" WREN asked. "I know how much you love him."

"I couldn't get him to stay," Mrs. Rison admitted. "He missed his old stomping grounds too much."

"This is probably the next step in becoming a crazy cat lady, but I'll keep him. He seems to really love Gracie."

"Wouldn't a cat wedding be grand? My grandson loves stuff like this. He's a wedding planner."

Wren smiled as Mrs. Rison gushed over her grandson, Adam. He was the one who bought Casper the rainbow collar. He was married to her ex-husband's brother Hannibal and they lived in New York

City. The old lady was immensely proud of him. He even had his own TV show on Cable.

"Anyway, I better go," said Wren. "You probably know about all the trouble we've been having in town."

"A murder!" Mrs. Rison exclaimed. "How ghastly! I used to be good friends with Garrett's father before he died. Garrett Senior loved Katie like a daughter, and she looked up to him like a father. Both father and son were such good people."

"You're right there." Wren thought for a moment. It wouldn't hurt to ask. "Is there anything you can tell me about the family? My dad is being accused of Garrett's murder and I need to prove him innocent. Anything you can tell me would help."

The line went quiet for a moment. Wren watched her two cats taking it in turns to eat from the food bowl. How polite.

"Brenda?" Wren asked. "Are you still there?"

"I shouldn't really gossip," said Mrs. Rison. "But I have nothing better to do." The old woman cleared her throat. "All I do know is that one day Garrett's father told me he was ashamed of Katie for something. It was about twenty-one, twenty-two years ago, I can't remember when. It was before the boy was born. The only reason I remember it is because I'd never seen him look so disappointed before."

"You think Katie did something bad?"

"I honestly couldn't say. I never did find out what it was. Anyway, I have to go. If Casper is staying with you, I'd like to get a new cat, maybe three. I don't like to have only my own thoughts for company."

They said goodbye, and Wren promised to visit once her father was cleared of murder, and she hung up. She had a lot to think about. What had Katie done that was so bad that she'd made her father-in-law ashamed of her?

"Where did the ginger cat come from?" Fiona asked, flitting into the kitchen.

"You must be color blind," said Wren. She slipped her cell back into her pocket. "The new cat is black."

Fiona shook her head and pointed. "No. Look. It's ginger."

The angel was right. There was another cat in her kitchen, sharing from the food bowl with both Gracie and Casper.

"Am I turning my house into a hostel for cats?" Wren exclaimed. She'd had enough. "Go on! Get out!"

All three felines made a run for it, exiting through the back-door cat flap. Wren tried to call Gracie back, but she wouldn't listen.

"So, what are we up to today?" Fiona asked. She removed a box of cereal from the cupboard and stared at the ingredients list. "Why is there so much sugar in this? Should you be buying this?"

"I made up a list of suspects last night," said Wren proudly. She took a sip from her half full coffee mug. It was cold. She liked cold coffee. "And we're going to talk to each and every one of them."

"Good idea."

"Though I am worried. What if someone attacks me? I know a little taekwondo, but what if it's not enough?"

They made breakfast, which was hardboiled eggs, a glass of grape juice, and two slices of toasted whole meal bread. Wren finished it off with two more cups of coffee and an apple.

"Have you heard anything from Jordan?" Fiona asked.

"Nothing," said Wren. "He must be devastated."

"Unless he killed Garrett."

"I'd like to believe he wouldn't kill his own father but I need to keep an open mind. My father's reputation depends on it."

She knew her father's reputation was already in tatters. His arrest was all over the county papers and local stations, though thankfully they hadn't revealed his criminal past. Sheriff Fisher must have worked hard to keep that information from the press. If the rest of the town knew what her parents used to do for a living, and that they'd been in jail, they'd be social pariahs.

"What does this mean for the two of you?" said Fiona.

"There is no two of us," Wren stated. "Or at least I don't think there is." She pondered their relationship before adding, "It's not as if I'm in love with him or anything. It's just lust." She looked out of the window, watching a slow cloud that looked like a clown drift by. "Is it lust? Is it love? I honestly don't know. All I do know is that he confuses me almost as much as he makes me feel special."

"Just don't drool all over him when we interrogate him."

Wren was about to suggest they head out when she noticed a set of keys on the edge of the kitchen table. It was the keys for the Metropolis. She really should have handed those into the police.

"I have an idea," said Wren. "There's some place we should stop off first."

Chapter 16

ain Street was always eerily quiet at eight in the morning.
Most businesses didn't open until at least nine or ten, and traffic was barely non-existent anyway. It was like walking through a ghost town.

"This reminds me of some of the Heavenly Suburbs," said Fiona. "It makes me sad."

They were walking past Van Clark's Coffee House. Veronica was sat behind a table, slamming her fingers angrily against a laptop keyboard. She looked frazzled. Was she working on the books?

"What are the Heavenly Suburbs?" Wren asked.

Fiona's world was utterly fascinating to her. Every morsel of information she found out about the afterlife made the universe seem that much bigger.

"It's sort of like a whole world with pre-built cities and parks and things like that," Fiona explained. "It's for people who did good in life, but not that good. It's sort of like a 3-star Heaven. It's nice enough, but...there's better."

"That sounds horrible. Who'd want to spend eternity in a place that's just okay?"

The angel shrugged. "I don't make the rules."

"Who does make the rules?"

Fiona ignored her as they arrived at the Metropolitan. Wren sighed, vowing to ask the question again later. The angel was reluctant to even say there was such a thing as a higher being.

"It smells of bleach in here," said Fiona as Wren unlocked the door. "But I can still smell blood as well."

They headed inside, and Wren locked the door behind her. She didn't want anyone wandering in while she was scoping the place out. They'd think she was planning a robbery.

Like father like daughter...

"Where do we start?" Fiona asked.

"We'll leave the crime scene until last," said Wren. "If I see the blood stains I might have a flashback."

Fiona grimaced. "Good idea."

"We'll try the back rooms. Dad said he heard a weird sound from back there when he was robbing the place. Perhaps there's something the police missed. Our local force isn't exactly CSI: Miami."

Wren tried not to look behind the counter as she headed for the inner door, but her grim curiosity took over. She looked.

"I think my breakfast is going to come up," she said, gagging.

"You did eat an awful lot," Fiona commented.

"I knew we were going to have a long day."

They headed through the door into the back passage. The carpet was brown and ancient, and the walls painted a grim mauve. It was like a dentist's waiting room. She expected to hear someone crying in terror as the dentist descended upon their open mouth with a drill.

"This is like Hell's waiting room," said Fiona with a shiver.

Wren couldn't help but laugh.

She headed into the break room as Fiona went into the bathroom. She didn't expect to find much in there.

"Wren!"

Jordan was on the small couch by the vending machine. He had blankets wrapped over him and his hair was stuck up all over the place.

"Are you sleeping here?" she asked.

He yawned. "I've got nowhere else to go, have I?"

"I'm pretty sure you live in one of the biggest houses in Snowflake Bay."

He shook his head. "Not anymore."

She watched him get up. He was wearing a baggy red t-shirt and a pair of extremely tight black boxer shorts. It was hard not to look, but she refrained herself. Jordan was going through a crisis. It would be wrong to leer.

"I want you to leave," he said, pulling on a pair of jeans.

"I can't leave," Wren insisted. She closed the door behind her. "My father is being accused of this crime."

"You're not a detective."

Wren knew she was going to hear that phrase a lot more. It was already starting to make her feel less confident. She knew she wasn't a detective, but did that mean she couldn't give it a try for her father's sake?

She crossed her arms. "Let's start with where you were on the night of the murder."

He sat by the small table in the room. "I've already told the police this."

"Tell *me*."

He looked tired and hungry. She figured he might be more responsive if he had something to eat. Wren ordered him a muesli bar from the vending machine and threw it to him. He caught it, opened the wrapper, and started eating.

"Well?" she demanded.

"I was at home all night in my bedroom," he answered.

Wren nodded. "Can anyone corroborate this?"

"My mom was downstairs. I could hear the clinking of wine glasses and her cursing when she couldn't get the cork out of a wine bottle."

He said it in such a deadpan manner that she almost laughed.

"Did she actually see you upstairs?" Wren asked.

"Not really." He finished his muesli bar and tossed the wrapper in the bin. Wren filled the kettle as he continued. "I'd already told her I wasn't speaking to her so she didn't bother me. I don't have an alibi but I didn't do it. I was angry with my father but not enough to kill him. What happened that day when I punched him...it was a misunderstanding. I regretted it later, but I never got a chance to make things up."

"Why did you punch him?"

"It's a family matter. I can't talk about it."

She filled two mugs with cheap instant coffee. Quite why they had this muck in the break room of a coffee house she had no idea. It would do for now.

"Did you tell the police?" asked Wren.

"They asked, but I just told them I got worked up because he refused to pay my tuition." He paused before adding, "It was a lie."

"Tell me the real reason you hit him. It might have something to do with your father's death."

"I'm not sure how."

"Please."

The kettle clicked, and Wren made the coffees and sat down at the table with them. Jordan sipped his and sighed with pleasure. He was obviously not used to the finer things in life. She refused to drink hers. It looked like garbage can water.

"Aarna got me this weird gift for Christmas," Jordan explained. "It was one of those DNA testing kits that trace back your ancestry"

"I did one of those," said Wren, smiling. "I found out I'm 4 percent Native American on my mother's side."

Jordan's stomach rumbled and a foul smell filled the air.

"Sorry," he said, blushing. "My fault."

"You do fart a lot," she admitted. "Though it's nothing to be ashamed of us. Everybody does it. I bet even Queen Elizabeth lets off a few times a day."

She went to open the window. It was really stiff, and so she pushed on it. It made an almighty squeaking, creaking sound that was so loud it could wake the dead.

Was that the noise my dad heard that night?

Someone was escaping the premises after the murder.

Jordan continued as the smell he'd created drifted away. "She bought one for herself, and she was upset when she got her results back. She had white Scottish ancestors. I decided it was finally time to do my test, just to take her mind off her own results."

"Why would Aarna be upset that she has Scottish ancestors?" Wren asked, not wanting to interrupt his flow, but curious.

"I think it's the white ancestor's thing. I don't think she was expecting it. Her parents come from a rich Indian family, and they consider whites to be beneath them. Not that Aarna is racist in any way." Jordan looked thoughtful for a moment. "Anyway, I sent my DNA off, along with that of my dad and mom too. I took some of their hair without asking. More samples help the results or something."

Wren had a horrifying feeling that she knew where this was going. She only hoped she was wrong.

"Garrett wasn't my biological father," Jordan revealed. The words seemed to pain him. She wanted to take his hand and comfort him but didn't think it was her place. "I got the phone call from the DNA ancestry place that day in the Metropolis. I was so angry I confronted him about it. I punched him. I accused him of always knowing but never saying anything. The truth was...the truth was he didn't know. He had no idea. He thought he *was* my biological father."

"It must have been a shock to him."

"I didn't give him time to respond. I just left, eventually ending up back home, where I confronted my mother about it. She told me some rubbish about a one-night stand while her and father were still dating and she didn't know who my bio Dad was. I didn't believe her and we argued. I really wanted to punch her too, if I'm honest." He looked ashamed at this admission. "She was so...so nasty."

Wren bit the bullet and reached across the table to take his hand. He pulled away.

"Katie came into the Metropolis later on and had a mighty row with Garrett," said Wren, pretending Jordan's rebuff never happened. "It was quite a show."

"Really?" said Jordan, surprised. "She never said."

"So, you don't know who your biological father is."

"No, but I'll find out. I'm sure she knows. She's just a liar."

Jordan suddenly started to cry. Wren did the decent thing and gave him a hug. She realized then and there that she didn't love him. He was attractive and he'd taken an interest in her after a very long romantic drought. She'd been flattered. There was nothing else to it.

"The DNA people told me something else," he admitted. His eyes were wide with fear now. "They said I have this inherited condition called familial adenomatous polyposis, or FAP. I don't really understand it yet, but it means I might be more at risk of developing bowel cancer."

"Oh Jordan," she said. "I'm so sorry."

"Things just keep getting better and better for me, right?"

He tried to kiss her.

"No," she insisted. It took everything she had to push him away. He really was very, very attractive. She would even say beautiful. "This has to stop."

"I need someone," he said.

"You need your family. Talk to your mom. Make her tell you the truth."

"You don't understand what a cold-hearted woman she is. It was like being brought up by a robot. My dad was the one who comforted me when I was upset, and talked to me, and raised me."

"She's just lost her husband. Be there for each other. Maybe things can change."

Wren hugged him again, gave him a chaste kiss on the cheek and left him to it. She had all she needed from Jordan for now – unless he was lying about who his real father was. Did he know? And could it have something to do with his father's death?

Fiona was waiting for her back in the coffee store. She was sitting at one of the tables, reading the menu. There was a box of pills on the table.

"I thought I'd leave you two to it," said Fiona.

"We had a good talk," said Wren. "I learned some juicy stuff."

Wren told her all about Jordan's father revelation, but it wasn't new to her. She seemed to know it all already.

"Why are you just nodding?" Wren asked, a little annoyed.

"The bathroom is right next to the break room," Fiona explained. "The walls are very thin, and there's an air circulation vent between the two rooms. I literally heard everything the both of you said." Fiona grinned at Wren's exasperated look. "Do you really think Katie doesn't know who Jordan's father is?"

"I don't know. She's next on our list." Wren picked up the bottle of pills. "Laxatives. Do you have anything to tell me?"

"I found these in the bathroom."

The morning that Garrett died Jordan had said his father had argued with Veronica over a bout of diarrhea with her customers. She'd accused him of sabotaging her business. Was this bottle of laxatives concrete proof that something shifty had gone on? Had Garrett spiked Veronica's coffee supply?

"I wouldn't have liked to be in Veronica's coffee shop bathroom that morning," Fiona quipped, trying not to laugh.

"This could've been serious," said Wren. "Someone could've had an adverse reaction to this stuff."

Fiona tapped the label on the side of the bottle. "This was issued to Katie Knowles last November. No wonder she's so cold. She was probably bunged up."

"Or she took laxatives to keep herself skinny. Yes, I can see that."

Wren was now more confused than ever. She was gaining information on her suspects at such a fast pace. It was hard to keep up with it all. She did know that Jordan hadn't killed his father. Or she thought she did.

What if he did kill him?

Jordan worked out. He had an incredible, muscular physique, which she could attest to personally. He would have the strength to knock his father to the floor and push the tremendously heavy coffee machine onto his head. Could a woman do that? Katie did yoga, she knew that much. She'd seen her once at the local yoga studio when she'd tried a class. Veronica certainly seemed capable. She had the wiry arms of an Olympic javelin thrower.

"Come on," said Wren, eager to get on with things. "Let's head off and interview Katie. I really want to know what she knows about Jordan's father."

"Don't you have an appointment this afternoon?" Fiona reminded her.

Wren felt the bile rise. "Oh. Cedric. I suppose I better go. I need him on our side so he gets his brother to represent Dad."

"Is Cedric's brother really worth it? You'll upset Reba."

It was worth anything to spare her father jail. She was sure Reba would understand. Family came first.

Chapter 17

There was some sort of commotion going on at the drag bar when Wren arrived. There were several drag queens gathered near the bar counter, pointing and shouting at each other. One of them even slapped another. Benedict entered the fray, in his male guise, and ended up with a knee to the groin for his troubles. When he saw Wren, he staggered over to greet her.

"I didn't know the drag game was so brutal," she commented, hiding a smirk.

"Are you kidding?" he said. The queens were still arguing. "Drag queens are some of the most brutal fighters I've ever met. You wouldn't want to get on their bad side."

"What's got them so rattled?"

"A wig went missing. You never, ever mess with a queen's wig."

He laughed, and she joined in. He had a nice smile, genuine and wide, showing his perfect white teeth.

Wren noticed Cedric sat at a table. "I'm here to meet him. Wish me luck."

"He used to be a regular you know," Benedict revealed.

"What?" Wren was shocked. "Since when?"

"He used to come in all the time until about three years ago. I heard he got sick or something. This is the first time I've seen Ceddy since then. Odd fellow, a bit laid back, a bit boring, but he always let his hair down when he was here. He used to have the time of his life. Tell him we miss him."

You learn something new every day.

"Benedict says he missed you," said Wren, sitting down at the table.

Cedric's face went bright red. "I liked it here. It felt like I wasn't pressured into meeting a woman and getting married. When I was here, I could just sit and have a drink."

This was a trait of Cedric she liked. So he had a fun side after all. What had happened? Benedict said he's been ill.

"Shall we eat?" Wren asked, her stomach rumbling. "I've not eaten anything since breakfast."

"They have this bacon burger/chicken burger combo here with onion rings that's to die for," said Cedric. "You have to try it."

Wren smiled. "Sounds delicious."

GARRETT'S HOUSE WAS a large, purpose-built building on the edge of town. It looked new, maybe twenty years old. It had three levels and a giant garage that could fit three cars. It was surrounded by acres of land, perfectly manicured grass with the occasional fir tree. It was quite stunning.

They must have quite a bit of money.

Fiona knocked on the large white door. A dog barked inside. After a while a drunken woman answered.

"Katie Knowles?" Fiona asked.

"I'm not buying anything," Katie said, her voice slurred. She was wearing obscene amounts of make-up. She looked like a clown. "Go away." She slammed the door.

How rude.

Fiona knocked again. Katie ignored her.

"Well that went well," Fiona mumbled.

BENEDICT SMILED DOWN at Cedric as he brought them their drinks. Cedric's mouth quirked in what Wren could only approximate was a smile in return. It was like he was embarrassed.

"How you keeping, Ceddy?" Benedict asked.

"I'm fine," Cedric answered stiffly. "Doing well."

"Keep it up," said Benedict, giving Wren a wink as he walked away.

She took a sip of her drink, some cocktail that Benedict had recommended called a "A Fruity Tuck." It was delicious.

"I'm afraid I have some bad news," said Cedric. He took a sip of his cocktail and spat it out. "That's horrid."

"Is it about your brother?" Wren asked.

"He was in a skiing accident in the Dolomites and can't make it," he explained with a hint of sadness. "He's going to be fine, but he has three broken ribs and a fractured pelvis. He's staying in a hospital in Italy for the foreseeable future."

"Oh. Right. I'm sure my dad's trial won't be for a while anyway. These kinds of things can take ages to get to court."

"I hope so."

She gulped down the rest of her drink, feeling hope leave her once again. Cedric's brother would've gotten her father off the burglary charges. What if Jackson didn't recover in time for the trial? Reba was a competent lawyer, but she wasn't a shark.

When the meal was served, all conversation died down. Wren didn't know what else to say. She just wanted to get out of there and find out how Fiona got on with Katie. The angel was a force to be reckoned with. She could make anybody talk.

Maybe she'd been an interrogator or something before she died.

"I know I put you off the other night," Cedric admitted. He was cutting up his burger into small pieces. It was weird. He did the same on their date the other night, like a mother cutting up dinner for a child. "I got embarrassed and then I started to be rude and I started talking about marriage and..."

"It's fine," said Wren. "It wasn't the best evening ever, but it certainly wasn't the worst."

"I think our second date is going a lot better than I'd hoped," said Cedric. He smiled at her. There was a bit of lettuce stuck in his teeth. "What do you think?"

Oh no, he thinks this is a date.

"This isn't a date," Wren stated. "I'm sorry if you think that."

Cedric gave a fake laugh. "I was just joking, trying to lighten the mood. You seemed so upset when I told you about my brother's accident."

"Did you even contact your brother? Has he even had an accident? Or is this all just a pretense to get me to go out with you again?" Cedric stared at her, not flinching. He wasn't giving anything away. "I can check you know. A lot of people know your brother in town. I'm sure one of them will tell me the truth."

"No. No." Cedric looked away. "He contacted me. He heard about it from one of the locals while he was on holiday. He was going to fly straight back until he skied over the edge of that cliff."

Wren was fed up. The meal had started out so well. She'd even started to like him after discovering he had a fondness for drag. It seemed any dinner she had with Cedric would end up turning sour, no matter what.

"Thank your brother for me," said Wren, calming down. There was an awful smell wafting over from Cedric. "It was a nice offer."

"I've ruined things again," Cedric admitted.

"Maybe we both ruined it, though it was mainly you."

Cedric stood up, looking panicked. "I have to use the bathroom. I'll see you later. Maybe?"

Before she could reply he had run off to the bathroom so fast he knocked his chair over and almost rugby tackled a drag queen. How very odd.

Did he soil himself?

"What is that smell?" Fiona asked.

"Never mind that," said Wren. She hadn't noticed the angel arrive. Had she walked in or flitted in? "Cedric's brother has had a skiing accident. He won't be able to be Dad's lawyer."

"Katie slammed the door in my face," said Fiona. She sounded disappointed. "I think she was drunk."

Fiona picked a leftover fry from off Cedric's plate. "We've both had a very productive day it seems."

It would do no good to sit there and moan about their lack of success. They had to be proactive if they wanted to find Garrett's murderer.

Chapter 18

Wren knocked loudly on Katie's front door. She wanted to sound like a police officer or a debt collector. She thought it would make Katie listen.

Katie opened the door a minute later.

"Are you trying to break my door?" Katie complained. She had a fizzing drink in her hand. It looked like Alka-Seltzer. "Go away!"

"My father is being accused of killing your husband and I know he didn't do it," said Wren quickly, hoping Katie wouldn't slam the door in her face. "Please. Talk to me. Help me find out who did it."

Katie sighed and put a hand to her head. "I have a hangover. Or I'm still drunk. Or both. I don't feel like talking. I just want to be alone."

"Please."

The woman stepped aside to let them come in. Wren was in for a shock. The inside of the house was immaculate, with marble flooring and oak paneled walls. Replicas of famous paintings hung on the wall and there was an even a crystal chandelier.

"How rich are you?" Wren asked.

I didn't mean to say that out loud.

"Garrett's father won the Lotto," Katie explained, leading them towards the lounge area. She was unsteady on her feet. "Fifty million or something. He left it all to my husband when he died. He was a stingy man so there was more or less the whole lot left when he carked it." Katie looked suddenly sad. "I haven't thought about Garrett Senior in a long time. I miss him."

She laughed again, all melancholic memories of her father-in-law forgotten, and sat down on a sleek white corner sofa. Wren and Fiona joined her, staring in awe around the room. There was another chandelier above them, sparkling like diamonds under the sun. The fireplace was marble. She felt like she was in a royal palace.

"What do you want to know?" Katie asked. She took some pills out of her snakeskin purse and swallowed them. They looked like the exact same bottle of laxatives that Fiona had found in the coffee shop. *That woman is going to be rushing off to the John very, very soon.* "I'm busy. I was supposed to be hosting a dinner party tonight. I won't be having that now, will I? I was looking forward to it." She sighed and rubbed at her head. "I have a headache coming on."

"I spoke to Jordan," said Wren. "He told me about the DNA test."

"Pillow talk?"

"No. No. He...He needed someone to talk to, and I was there. You know he's sleeping at the coffee shop?"

"He won't even look at me. He called me a slut and said I ruined his life and now he might have cancer because I wasn't truthful with him." She smiled sadly. "He's right. I am a slut and I did ruin his life. I should have told him long ago about his biological father. I should have told Garrett. It's just...the lie was just to easier to maintain, and I didn't want them to look at me like they hated me, like Garrett Senior looked at me when he found out."

There was a portrait of the family on the wall above the fireplace. It was huge, dominating the wall. Jordan appeared to be about ten, and Katie had her original nose. The three of them looked so happy.

"What made you tell your husband such a lie?" Fiona asked crossly.

"I didn't know he wasn't Jordan's father," Katie admitted. She appeared to be gradually sobering up. Her words were less slurred, though her hands still shook a little. "Not at first. When Jordan was two he had a serious fall and hit his head. He lost a lot of blood. I donated mine for a transfusion, but not before I found out that my son and husband had different blood types. It meant he couldn't possibly be Jordan's biological father."

"You had an affair," Fiona accused her.

Wren nudged Fiona. She was being judgy. If they wanted Katie opened up, then they had to stay neutral.

"I had an affair," Katie admitted. She genuinely looked ashamed of her actions. "I wasn't proud of myself, but it happened, and I couldn't take it back. I wouldn't take it back. That affair gave me Jordan, and he made my life complete. Do you know what it was like growing up in the foster system? I had no one. I was so desperate for someone to love me and I finally had it. Well, there was a husband before Garrett, but I divorced him because he got on my nerves."

"Who did you have an affair with?" Wren asked.

"It was after Garrett's mother died and Garrett Senior moved in with us." Katie looked away. "That man was like a father to me. I genuinely loved him. He made me feel part of the family. For someone who'd never had that it was a dream come true."

Wren briefly thought that maybe Garrett Senior was Jordan's father, but that didn't make sense.

"After his mom's funeral service ,Garrett and I went out drinking. We had a little argument, and he left me at the nightclub we'd ended up at. As the night wore on I got very, very drunk. I even thought I saw my odious ex-husband at one point, but I scared him off. I can vaguely remember having sex with someone in a public toilet but that's about it. I can't remember their face. I wish I could. I really wish I could."

Wren believed her. She genuinely didn't know whom she'd had that rendezvous with. She couldn't imagine how awful that must be. Jordan's father could be anyone. Jordan could have served his father at the coffee shop dozens of times and not even known. Katie must have thought the man she slept with was the man walking past her,or sat next to her on the bus.

"Garrett Senior caught me sneaking back in that night," Katie went on. "He saw the look on my face and he knew. He just knew. He was never the same with me after that."

"Did you kill your husband?" Wren asked calmly.

"I loved him," Katie stated after a brief flicker of anger. "If anything, he had reason to kill me. I was the one who cheated and spent all his money and shouted at him all the time."

"Where we you at the time of the murder?" Fiona asked.

"I was here. Jordan was upstairs, sulking. I drank a bit. Watched some TV. Drank a bit more. Went to bed. Woke up and drank a bit more." Katie laughed. "I think I passed out after that."

Wren nodded. "Can anyone corroborate that you were here?"

"I ordered a meal at about eleven. It came at half past. The Italian place in town really does a wonderful vegan spaghetti Bolognese."

"Perhaps you killed him because he threatened to leave you and you didn't want to be on your own," Fiona suggested.

"I just told you I was here all night," Katie snapped. "I was picking out wallpaper samples! I wanted to change the décor in the spare room. Garrett loved his lavender." She smirked. "Stupid color."

"Or perhaps you wanted your husband's money all to yourself." Fiona seemed smug, which rubbed Wren up the wrong way. She'd never this unpleasant side of the angel before. "There must be millions of that Lotto money left that he inherited from his father." Katie was about to interrupt but Fiona continued. "Or perhaps you didn't want your husband to find out who the real father of Jordan was and you killed him to shut him up. Or maybe he did know who the real father was and you killed him to keep him quiet. Or maybe..."

"Stop it!" Katie cried. "Just stop it!"

Fiona had the decency to look ashamed. Wren reminded herself to have a word with her later.

"Sorry about that," said Wren. "She's overeager. She doesn't want Wick to go to jail for something he didn't do."

"Who is she?" Katie asked. She was starting to become hostile again, which Wren didn't want. They'd have to leave soon. "I've never seen her before. What does she have to do with any of this?"

Wren looked at Fiona, unsure what to say.

A small dog scampered in and leapt upon Katie's lap. It was some sort of Pomeranian. It looked like a giant ball of dust and fluff with eyes. It yapped a few times before Katie took a small bag of treats from her purse and fed him what appeared to be tiny buttons of dry beef.

"Jordan has cut me out of my life, and my husband is dead," said Katie piteously. "This little one is all I have left."

Wren and Fiona left her to her grief. It felt wrong to intrude when she was so clearly having such a bad time. Besides, Wren thought she had all the information she needed for now. Katie didn't kill her husband.

Probably.

When they were outside Wren turned to Fiona. "Why were you so hostile?" she demanded.

"That woman cheated on her husband," Fiona replied. "I was taught that cheating was a sin. This so-called modern society embraces sin. I don't like it."

"I'd say she's paid the price for her sin."

"She had a man she loved and who loved her and she almost blew it by having drunk sex in a public bathroom! It's disgusting. I never would've cheated on my husband like that, and I had offers, believe me. I was away from my husband and I was lonely and I had offers and I could have..." Fiona looked away. "Anyway, I've said too much. I'm not supposed to talk about my past. Let's just go home for now. I'm tired and angry and I just want to get away from all these awful people."

Fiona flitted away, leaving Wren standing there, gob smacked.

FIONA FOUND HERSELF in Wren's back garden. Gracie and her two cat friends were chasing each other around, having a whale of a time. She didn't know how cats kept up that levels of energy day by day. Being an angel was draining.

"How could I have revealed so much about myself?" she asked the cats. "Juniper will be so angry with me."

I'm angry at myself.

She decided to go and spend the night back at her apartment in Golden. She needed a little time away from this situation with Wren and the murder. It was too much, too emotional. Maybe tomorrow she could be less judgmental about the people they were interviewing.

"No," she said defiantly. "I have a right to an opinion. If I think Katie Knowles was a selfish whore, then she's a selfish whore."

How could Katie be like that? She had everything. She had a husband and money and a house to live in. Back when Fiona died, all she had was a top bunk bed at the army barracks in East London. Her husband and infant son were in another country. She was being paid peanuts. She felt out of place and lonely. But she didn't complain. She was doing her duty as a nurse and a human being. She was proud of it.

I need Brock.

She tried to flit away but it wouldn't work. All her flitting allocations must have been used up today. "Looks like it's just you and me," she told Gracie, who was now sitting at her feet, looking up at her with a confused expression. The other cats were sat on the table under the gazebo, watching her warily, unsure. "Am I being too judgmental? Or do I just have standards?"

A hand grasped her shoulder. Fiona screamed.

"Sorry," muttered Cedric. "I didn't mean to startle you."

Fiona pushed him onto the grass. "Stay away from me!"

"I was just checking on Wren," said Cedric, pulling himself to his feet. "We didn't have a very good time this afternoon and I wanted to give her a gift to say I'm sorry." He held out a box of chocolates so big you could park a car in it. "Here. Give this to her."

"Oh. You must be Cedric. You startled me." She took the box of chocolates from him. "Thank you."

"You're very beautiful. Your hair shines like an angel."

Fiona blushed. "You flatter me."

He smiled and walked away. Fiona watched him leave, making sure he was out of sight before she ripped open the box of chocolates and started eating them. They were very good, and more than enough to make her feel better again. It didn't hurt to be flattered by a man either.

What was Wren complaining about? Cedric is so nice!

Chapter 19

There was a police car parked across the road from Katie's house. Sheriff Fisher was sitting in the driver's seat, watching her with scorn. Wren marched over to him and got in the passenger side. The inside was like an ice box. Did he never turn the heating on?

"Why are you watching Katie's house?" she asked.

The inside of the car smelled like stale burgers and fries. Sheriff Fisher looked like he hadn't slept in a week. He had bags under his eyes the size of an elephant's foot.

"Why are you talking to Katie?" the sheriff demanded.

"I was just giving her my condolences," said Wren, trying to keep the defensive tone out of her voice. "She's just lost her husband. She needs all the support she can get at a time like this. I know how she feels."

"Your husband didn't die. He's still alive."

She hated the fact that everyone in Snowflake Bay knew of her marriage break-up. Nobody outside of her family had the precise facts, but they knew enough. It was still idle gossip all these years later.

"How well do you know Katie?" Wren asked, changing tack. "I know you were friends with Garrett."

"I know she loved Garrett and would never kill him," the sheriff replied. "She's a remarkably kind, caring woman."

Wren almost choked on her own saliva. "Really? That's not the impression she gives off to everyone else. She's haughty and hostile and rude to everyone."

"That's just a veneer. You don't know her like I do. She loved Garrett."

The sheriff's eye twitched slightly, and the corner of his mouth was curled up in a smile. Was he in love with Katie?

Was he Jordan's father?

"Were you sleeping with Katie?" Wren spat out.

The sheriff glared angrily at her. "Get out of my car."

"You're not saying no," said Wren. "Why is that?"

She crossed her arms and refused to leave. This was too important. She had to have all the facts.

"I am not having an affair with Katie," he stated. "Happy now?"

"I'm not sure I believe you," said Wren. "I saw that look in your eye when you talked about her. That was love."

"Is this any of your business?"

"It is my business if the man charging my father with murder is the man who framed him in the first place!"

He got out of the car and charged around to her side. He opened the door. The anger coming from him was so palpable he was almost steaming.

"Get out of my car now before I drag you out," he screamed.

She was scared now. "Is this a confession?"

"I don't answer to you, but no, this isn't a confession."

"Where...where were you at the time of the murder?"

He didn't answer her, and so she refused to get out of the car. He was a trustworthy man. She'd known him all her life. Wren was sure she'd believe whatever he told her.

"I'm waiting," she said impatiently.

"I was binge watching *Call the Midwife* with Keegan if you must know," the sheriff admitted. "Keegan came around because it was my birthday the day before and he'd forgotten. He brought some terrible chocolate cake he'd made himself and we caught up with the last season of *Call the Midwife* on Netflix."

"That's nothing to be ashamed of. I love *Call the Midwife*."

She got out of the car, careful to avoid the sheriff. His heated stare made her feel very uncomfortable. Maybe she deserved it for accusing him of murder.

Or maybe I accused the right man?

"I'm sorry," said the sheriff. His face softened. "I'm sorry if I scared you. I do have a temper."

Wren was wary as she said, "I did accuse you of murder."

"Garrett was my best friend. I was just checking in on his wife. I promised myself that nothing bad would ever happen to her."

"But you are in love with her, right?"

He didn't answer her. She left it at that.

FIONA WAS SITTING OUT on the front porch. There was a pitcher of sweet tea on a table and she was drinking from a glass. Gracie was sat on her lap, looking relaxed and smug. Moths attacked the small light bulb that hung from the ceiling. It looked very cozy.

"What took you so long to get home?" Fiona asked.

Wren sat down and sighed with relief. "Today has been a very long day."

She poured herself some sweet tea. It was her own concoction. She bought plain powdered tea and added to it, creating new recipes. This one was strawberry and apple, made from real fruit juices. It was the only way she could make something like that and know it didn't have any cloying sweeteners in it like most store-bought sweet teas did.

"I bumped into Sheriff Fisher," said Wren. "He's in love with Katie, and I don't think he killed Garrett."

"Love can make you crazy," said Fiona. "I wouldn't believe a word he says, sheriff or not."

Wren nodded. "Yeah, I know. As much as it pains me to admit it, despite his alibi, he's still on my suspects list, as is Katie and Jordan. They're all liars, and they all have possible motives to kill Garrett. Katie has several motives, as you pointed out so bluntly." She grinned at Fiona's outrageous look and took a sip of her tea. "I'm not sure about Jordan. He had no motive to kill his father as far as I'm aware. Maybe he killed him because he was so upset the man wasn't his biological father? Maybe his emotions finally got to him? Jordan is a very passionate person." She took another sip of tea to hide her blush. "Sheriff Fisher is so very in love with Katie. Maybe he finally decided he wanted her to himself and murdered his best friend. I'd like to think he was a law-abiding person and wouldn't do anything so heinous, but anyone can be forced to murder by circumstance."

Fiona stroked Gracie's head. "You sound like you know by experience."

"Someone wronged me badly in the past, and... I thought about hurting them. I would never have gone through with it, but I was so devastated and angry that I couldn't see reason. Maybe I could've killed them. I don't know."

The angel poured herself another glass of tea and waited patiently. Wren wanted to share her story. She *needed* to share it.

125

Chapter 20

"I used to work at the local tourism office," said Wren. She leaned back into her chair, anxious. Her past was a mixture of joy and sadness. "Snowflake Bay has a lot of tourism because of all the movies and TV shows they filmed here. I say used to film here. We don't get that many big Hollywood productions anymore, but the Trademark Channel films a couple of Christmas movies here every year. You should see the town dressed up as Christmas in the middle of Summer! So, the tourism is quite high, and the local council decided to open up a tourist office. I got my first job there, straight out of school. Even back then I was directionless. I didn't know what I wanted to do with my life. But I liked my new job. It gave me money, and new friends, and I enjoyed taking tourists around the town to show them all the places they'd seen on film.

"I made a really good friend in Penny."

Fiona held her hand up. "Who's Penny?"

"She works at the tourist office. Anyway, Penny and I had wonderful fun. We sometimes did tours together and stayed late after work getting drunk. It was during that time I was with Alex. We'd been dating since we were thirteen, can you believe it? He proposed during senior Prom, and we married a month later. I didn't regret a thing. I knew I loved him and wanted to spend the rest of my life with him. My parents loved him too. They treated him like a second son.

"My boss at the travel agency was Gregory Pendle. He was fine to work with, though he could be quite strict at times. I got on great with him. I'd been there about seven years when he cornered me in his office and kissed me. I told him I wasn't interested and he apologized and I thought everything was fine. It turned out he was harboring a grudge that boiled up over the next couple of years."

"What did he do?" Fiona asked.

Wren felt her hands tremble as she gripped her glass of sweet tea. "He told Alex that we were sleeping together. I can still see the look on Alex's face now, all that hurt and betrayal. I convinced him that Gregory was lying, and I was sure we'd worked it out, but after that things were never the same. I had it out with Gregory over his lies and he fired me.

"Alex and I tried to carry on as normal for months, but he'd lost trust in me, and I felt betrayed because he initially believed Gregory. Then I found out he'd kissed someone else. He admitted to it and he felt guilty about it, but after that I didn't trust him. After a while we decided we couldn't live together without trust and we split up."

Fiona reached over the table to grip her hand. The angel's fingers were tiny.

"That's terrible," said Fiona. "But how did this lead to you contemplating murder? Was it Alex you wanted to kill?"

"No. I never blamed him. I blamed Gregory." Wren hated even saying his slimy name. It was like molten lava on her tongue. "After Alex left and we started divorce proceedings I needed a job, and so I sucked down my pride and went back to the tourism office. Gregory seemed repentant over what he did, and he apologized, and so I got over it. It was nice to work with Penny again.

"Then Penny told me she was the one who Alex kissed, and she told me they were thinking about dating each other but didn't want to upset me. I gritted my teeth and gave them my blessing. Inside I wanted to scratch her eyes out. But I didn't. Alex could date whomever he wanted.

"Then Gregory tried it on again. I told him to get lost again. He apologized again. This time I'd had enough. His lies last time had ruined my marriage and I wasn't having it. So I sued him for sexual harassment."

Fiona opened her mouth in shock.

"It turned out the tourism office was owned by a subsidiary of the Trademark Channel. They didn't want a scandal, and they didn't want the town to pull out of letting them film there, and so they settled outside of court. I got a million dollars."

"What about Gregory?" Fiona asked. "I hope he got fired."

Wren laughed bitterly. "Nope. He still works there, but he's on a very tight leash."

She took another sip of her tea but found the glass empty. The pitcher was empty too.

"There's my tale," said Wren. "I got a million dollars, but I lost my husband."

"What happened with him and Penny?" Fiona asked delicately.

"It didn't last long. She still works at the tourism office. I hear she has a worse love life than I do."

"So, you're not still friends?"

"Never in a million years."

They watched the moths circle the light bulb, hitting the hot glass, chasing each other, playing games. The night was getting cold.

"You never said who you wanted to kill," said Fiona.

"I thought that was obvious," said Wren. "I wanted to kill Gregory."

"The son of a bitch might have deserved it."

"Possibly, but it made me feel so guilty for even thinking it. The hate I felt for that man made me a lesser person. I like to think I've gotten over it but talking about him even now makes me hate him."

Sometimes she saw him in town. He would smile and say hello and act like everything was fine between them. She would ignore him. She didn't think she'd be able to stop herself from throttling him if she engaged him in conversation.

Some time after I told my parents about it, Gregory's house was broken into and his house completely trashed. Was that Dad? Or Mom?

She found herself smirking. Perhaps Gregory deserved it.

"So, what about you?" Wren asked. She'd had enough of talking about her pathetic past. "You keep letting bits and pieces of your life slip out. I know you were married."

"I'm not supposed to talk about it," Fiona insisted.

"You can be vague. Talk to me. If you're going to be staying with me for the foreseeable future, then I want to know you."

Fiona continued to stroke Gracie's head. Wren sensed a deep sadness in her, a grief that hadn't settled.

"I was married once, but I died," said Fiona. "He was the kindest, gentlest man in the whole world, but he could also be brave and pig headed and he had the smelliest feet. He could make the pig sty seem fragrant by comparison. But I loved him, and I died, and I could never say goodbye."

"When did you die?" Wren asked. "Or is that too sensitive?"

"I really can't tell you. Sorry."

Wren sighed. She'd get some private information out of her eventually. For now, she'd let the angel keep her secrets.

"Tell me about the afterlife then," said Wren. "How does one become an angel?"

"If you do good in life you get given a choice; go to Heaven, or become an angel. I chose Heaven at first, but then I got bored, and I asked to become an angel."

"Who asks you?" Wren wondered. "Is it God?"

"No. It's another senior angel called Gabriel. He's sort of like the boss of all angels. Imagine...imagine a small-town mayor crossed with a bossy librarian. He's nice enough, but only in small doses." Fiona laughed. Gracie became startled and jumped from her lap and ran back into the house. "He tells really filthy jokes."

"Can I ask why you got bored with Heaven? Surely it's the most wonderful place in existence?"

"Well of course it's wonderful, but that can get repetitive after a while. I lasted about twenty years before I left my little slice of Heaven and decided to become an angel." She appeared thoughtful. "Heaven was nice. Really nice. But I was made to help people, and I can't do that by lounging around all day."

"Sounds good to me."

"The boredom can drive people insane, and so they have their memories wiped and start the process all over again. I didn't want that to happen to me."

The angel looked up into the starry sky, lost in thought. There was an awful lot she wasn't revealing, but Wren could wait. They'd only known each other for a few days, even though it felt like they'd been best friends for life.

"Why do I feel like we're best friends already?" Wren asked. "We've only known each other three days."

"I'm such a wonderful person," said Fiona.

"It's not that some weird angel magic like what happened with Keegan?"

Fiona shrugged. "I don't know what went on there. But as for me and you...I've never really had a proper friend before. It feels right."

Wren couldn't agree more.

THE SNORING BURSTING forth from Fiona's room was almost rattling the floorboards. It didn't make sense that angels could snore. Surely a person's every ailment was healed the moment someone died?

There were three cats on her bed.

"Why do you think you can just waltz in here and take over?" she demanded. "What is wrong with you?"

Gracie looked up at her, sleepy eyed and adorable. She meowed gently, licked the ear of the black cat, and went back to sleep. The ginger cat's ear twitched, obviously listening in and pretending to rest.

"I'll have to put up some posters around the neighborhood," she said, slipping into her dressing gown. She was going to read a little before she switched her light off. "Before I know it there'll be half a dozen of you little felines in my home!"

She laughed and went to close the curtains. A reflection of light caught her eye from the bushes in her front garden.

Binoculars?

Wren opened the window. "Get off my property before I call the police!"

Something rustled in the bushes and then all was still. Wren watched, eyes alert, for another minute before sighing with relief. They were gone.

Someone is spying on me...

She closed the window and pulled her curtains closed. She'd never felt so scared in all her life.

Chapter 21

Fiona tapped on the window, making cute baby noises. Wren had stopped the ginger cat from coming in that morning, and now it was outside on the windowsill, meowing and looking pathetic. She was determined. It could find somewhere else to sleep. Two cats were more than enough.

"Let the poor thing in," said Fiona. "He's hungry."

"I'm not in the mood for this," Wren snapped. She sipped at her coffee, feeling anxious. "Some other sucker can feed it."

"You let the other one stay."

Wren fixed the angel with her direst stare. "I'm doing Mrs. Rison a favor. I wasn't happy about it, but Casper seems to like it here."

"So does the other one."

Wren sat by the table and poured herself a coffee. She added milk and three spoons of sugar to it.

"Why are you in such a foul mood this morning?" Fiona asked. "I thought we got on great last night."

"Someone was watching the house," said Wren. "I caught them spying on me with binoculars. They were hiding in the bushes in the front garden."

"Maybe it was an owl or something. The light from the moon reflects from their eyes."

During the night Wren had tried to convince herself of the same thing. It had to have been an owl, or a candy wrapper that had blown onto her garden. Why would someone be watching her?

"It's the killer," said Wren. She knew with certainty. "They spray painted that message on my house, which is still there by the way because I haven't gotten around to cleaning it off yet, and now they're watching me. They want me to stop investigating Garrett's murder." She grinned and stood up. Nobody was going to make her feel low or anxious ever again. "Fat chance of that. I'm heading into this to the bitter end."

"Good on you," said Fiona. "But first..."

THERE WERE FOOTPRINTS in the soil behind the bush. Wren hadn't just seen an owl. Someone *had* been watching the house. Fiona couldn't help but shiver. This investigation was starting to get sinister.

"Maybe the postman left them," Fiona suggested.

"What is the postman doing behind my bushes?" Wren demanded.

The angel sighed. "Someone was watching the house, weren't they? This is making me feel sick. My wings are tingly. To think that someone is..."

Fiona felt an odd sensation on her back. Before she knew it, her wings had sprouted, fully formed, almost knocking Wren to the ground.

"Oh dear!" she said, panicking. "What's going on? Someone is going to see!"

She flitted inside the house before she could start a full-scale panic. She tried to push her wings back inside her body but they wouldn't budge.

What's going on? This has never happened before!

"What are you thinking?" Wren cried, coming back inside the house. "Someone could have seen you!"

"It happened involuntarily!" Fiona protested. "I just got so anxious that they sprouted without me willing them to."

"Try to calm down and maybe they'll disappear, or go back inside your body, or wherever your wings go when they're not here."

"They can sprout in and out of my body in a single moment. All I have to do is will them."

"Then do it."

Fiona nodded, pushing aside all thoughts of sinister killers watching her every movement. She thought about Brock's beautiful eyes, and her baby son, and the wonderful time she'd had last night with Wren. There were a lot more positives than negatives in her life.

"It's working," said Wren. "They're shrinking!"

Fiona smiled as her wings vanished back inside her body. She spun around, trying to see what was going on, and fell into the couch.

"Crisis averted," said the angel. "Thank goodness."

"Has that ever happened before?" Wren asked.

"Not really," said Fiona. "But I haven't had my wings for that long either. I'm learning something new every day."

Nobody had told her this could happen during training. Then again, training had been very brief. They'd told her she'd learn more on the job than from boring lessons. Maybe she was. Or maybe she was just terrible at her job? Wren's life was actually *worse* now. There weren't murders and threats and stalkers before this pint-sized angel turned up.

"How long have you been an angel exactly?" Wren asked carefully.

Fiona averted her gaze. "A year, give or take six months, but I've worked hard. This was just a... just a nervous reaction to something. I bet even Gabriel loses control if he gets startled by a centipede."

"You didn't act like this when we found that threat on the door."

Wren was right. She'd been shaken, but had more or less accepted it. Why had this been so different? Why had the thought of someone spying on the house caused such a reaction in her?

"Oh Fiona..."

"I don't like the thought of someone watching me," snapped Fiona. "It makes me feel unsafe." She paused before adding, "I had a stalker once, okay? It was when I was married. This stalker made my life very difficult, and the police didn't take my concerns seriously. I was very scared."

"What happened?"

"My husband beat him up and that was the last of it." Fiona shivered. "Just leave it, okay? I don't really like talking about it. My pre-angel life is behind me now."

"LET'S JUST FINISH BREAKFAST and get on with our day," said Wren, wanting to change the subject. The angel really did seem rattled. She obviously had more to tell when the time was right. "I want to go and see Veronica this morning. She's probably hoping to take advantage of the Metropolis being shut down, but I won't let that stop me from quizzing her."

She was about to head back into the kitchen when her phone rang. It was Jordan.

"Can I ask you a favor?" he asked.

"Sure," she answered.

"I'm opening up the Metropolis today, but I need some help. You'd be forever in my debt if you agreed to work with me full time."

There was a flirting lilt to his voice that he must know made her crumble. The man could turn any sentence into a come on.

I bet even his eyes are flirting with me.

"Don't you need to be organizing your father's funeral?" Wren asked.

"They're not releasing the body until they've found the killer," Jordan explained. "Please, Wren. The Metropolis was my father's dream. I don't want it to see go to wrack and ruin or have Veronica's lame coffee shop get all his customers."

Wren looked towards Fiona, pleading for help. She'd put the call on speaker so the angel could hear everything. Fiona shrugged.

"Fine," said Wren, relenting, though not because of his sexy voice. "I'll be about half an hour, but I need an hour off for lunch. I have things to do."

"That's fine." He went quiet for a moment. "Thank you for this. Like I said, you'll be forever in my debt for this."

He hung up, and Wren couldn't help but smile. His final line had been more than flirting. It was almost erotic.

By the end of today I'm going to be in bed with him again, aren't I? I won't be able to control myself.

"You're almost drooling," said Fiona.

"You heard that, right?" she asked. "He was flirting."

Wren nodded. "He really was."

"And now that he's taking over the Metropolis full time he might not be going back to college. Could the two of us actually have a future?"

She couldn't let herself get too excited. Things had a way of turning sour where her life was concerned. Besides, why would Jordan give up a promising career in law just to run a coffee shop?

Why would he give up every glamorous woman in the world to marry a divorcee with bad hair, criminal parents, and no ambition?

"You're thinking about how terrible you are," Fiona stated.

"It's my default mode," Wren admitted.

Fiona sighed with exasperation and headed into the kitchen. Wren contemplated phoning Jordan back and telling him she couldn't come in, but she knew she wouldn't. She was starting to run out of money, and a job had literally landed on her doorstep. She couldn't afford to turn it down, Jordan or no Jordan.

Yes. I'm going in because I need a job, and not because Jordan will be there.

She thought she'd sorted out her feelings for Jordan yesterday. How had one single conversation brought her right back to the beginning again?

"Hello?" a voice called.

Damn. I left the front door open.

"I'm glad I caught you before you went to work or whatever it is you do all day," said Reba, just waltzing in. She had a plastic bag full of paper files with her. "I need to talk to you about your father's case."

Wren gritted her teeth and smiled. It was too early in the day to be dealing with such a morning person.

"Would you like a coffee?" Wren offered.

Reba pulled a face. "Dear Heavens, no. I haven't had caffeine in ten years. It makes me so hyper I almost start flying about the place. I'll just have a blueberry tea." At Wren's baffled look she opened her purse and took out a small purple packet. "Here. I have some. You should try it. Blueberries are a superfood."

They entered the kitchen, Reba making herself at home.

"Your father has quite the past," said Reba, sipping her tea. It did smell quite fragrant. "I've made hard copies of everything. I thought you might like to have a look at them. See what kind of man he used to be."

"I'm not sure I want to know," Wren admitted.

"It's not that bad," said Reba, glancing at Fiona, who was staring at her. "Do I have something on my face?"

Fiona laughed. "Of course not."

The angel smiled and exited to the back garden. Wren wondered what was wrong with her. Why had she been acting so weird around Reba?

"Can I ask a question?" said Wren.

"Of course," said Reba.

"How did none of the family know about my parents and their criminal past? It doesn't make sense."

"From what my dad told me, your dad left home when he was sixteen with Aunt Dot and didn't return to Snowflake Bay until after he got out of prison. Of course, they don't know he was in prison. I promised Uncle Wick I wouldn't say anything."

"Why did he leave home?"

Reba shrugged. "Dad didn't know." She finished the last of her blueberry tea and stood up. "Right. I need to go and see Judge Popovar. I'm going to try and get Uncle Wick bail. Fingers crossed."

Reba gave her an air kiss and left. Wren looked at the bag full of files on the table. What secrets would they reveal about her mother and father? What crimes had he actually been arrested for?

She took the bag and headed outside. Fiona was sat under the gazebo with Gracie, Casper and the ginger cat.

"I don't need to know," she said, dumping the files into the paper recycling bin.

She knew who her father was now. He was a good man who'd done stupid things. His past deserved to stay in the past.

"Has she gone?" Fiona called out.

Wren sat by Fiona. It was chilly outside without a coat on. She could see her breath. Winter always came early in Snowflake Bay, sometimes bypassing Fall altogether. Pretty soon there would be snow. Dad always liked to make a bet on whether they'd have a white Christmas or not. She only hoped being arrested put him off this particular holiday tradition.

If he doesn't end up in jail, anyway.

"Why did you act so weird with Reba?" Wren asked.

"I wasn't acting weird," said Fiona defensively. "I was still a bit jumpy after my wings sprouted out like that. I was afraid it would happen again."

The ginger cat leapt onto her lap and started to make itself comfortable. Wren smiled and gave it a cuddle. Gracie gave her a brief look of jealousy before going back to sleep again.

"Am I doing something to attract all these cats?" Wren asked.

"I think they're just drawn by your kindness," said Fiona.

"Perhaps I'm too kind," Wren admitted.

WREN WATCHED THROUGH the window, uncertain whether to head inside. Jordan was wiping the tables down, singing an Ed Sheeran song. His eyes were red from crying, but he was trying to keep himself upbeat. Her feelings for him were seriously doing her head in.

"Hey," she said, opening the door. "The coffee shop never looked so clean!"

His wide smile made her feel ten times better. "I've been at it all night. Dad would've hated seeing the dust and mess."

"Can we talk for a bit?"

"Sure. Take a seat."

She sat down, uncertain what she was going to say. She knew she had to say something.

"Are you okay?" he asked, sitting down.

"What do you feel for me?" she asked.

She felt like a monster for asking him this question while he was going through a traumatic time, but she had to ask. How would she ever know?

He looked confused. "I don't understand."

"We go to bed, and it's great, and but that's pretty much it. We don't talk. We don't go on dates. What are we?"

Jordan was about to answer when something smashed through the window. A brick hit the back of Wren's head and she screamed in pain as she was propelled from her chair onto the floor. For a brief second she thought she'd been shot.

What the...

"Veronica!" Jordan shouted.

Wren looked up to see Veronica Van Clark stood outside, staring in horror at what she'd caused.

Chapter 22

"I'm so sorry," Veronica wailed. "I didn't mean to hit you."

Jordan was carefully wrapping a bandage around Wren's forehead. There was a small gash, and it hurt a bit, but it wasn't bad, and it had already stopped bleeding. It certainly didn't require a trip to the hospital, which Veronica was insisting on. She was probably afraid she was going to get sued.

"Why did you do it?" Wren asked.

Veronica glared daggers at Jordan. "I had the water in my coffee machine tested, and they found traces of laxatives."

"Why would you think I did it?" Jordan demanded.

A guilty look crossed Jordan's face. It was brief, but Wren saw it. She knew then that he'd sabotaged Veronica's business. Was it on his father's orders, or had he done it on his own? Either way it wasn't good.

"Either you or your father did it," Veronica accused.

"Does it matter?" Jordan asked her. "My father is dead."

"It matters to me. Now nobody will come into my store because they think they'll never leave the toilet if they do!"

Wren didn't know whether to intervene or stay silent. It was none of her business. Maybe this was the perfect time to talk to Veronica?

"I'm sorry," said Jordan. "I only did it to help my father."

"How horrible!" Veronica cried. "You will buy me a new coffee machine."

Jordan nodded. "I promise. I really am sorry."

Veronica shrugged. "I believe you."

Now that the laxative mystery was solved...

"Can you leave us for a bit to talk?" Wren asked Jordan.

He looked confused, but said, "I suppose. I'll just do a quick stock check or something."

After he'd left them to it, Wren checked her bandages. It was wrapped quite expertly. If the law career didn't work out, then Jordan had a backup in nursing.

"Does it hurt?" Veronica asked. "I really am sorry."

"It's fine," said Wren, secretly wanting to throw the brick back at her. "What I wanted to talk about was Garrett. What kind of relationship did the two of you have?"

"We didn't have one. We were rival business owners."

"But everyone more or less knows everyone else in this town. Surely you knew him before you decided to set up a brand new coffee shop barely five minutes' walk away from his already established business?"

The woman looked like she was about to make a run for it. Wren prepared to follow her, though she probably wouldn't be much good. Her head was hurting far worse than she'd let on.

"If you must know, we were in school together," Veronica admitted. "The same class and everything. We weren't friends, but we were friendly to each other when the occasion called for it."

"Garrett must have been really hot back then," said Wren.

Veronica smiled dreamily. "Oh yes, he certainly was. He was Prom King and star quarterback and school jock, but he wasn't arrogant. He was humble. He was quite intelligent too, which rubbed quite a few people the wrong way. Good looking *and* smart? We can't have that!" She realized she must have been smiling too much because she suddenly stopped and cleared her throat. "That's the extent to our relationship. I said hello to him, he said hello to me. That's about it."

Wren didn't need to be Cupid to know a look of love when she saw it. Veronica had it bad.

"You were in love with him," Wren accused. "You still are."

Veronica backed away, horrified. "Are you serious? Don't be stupid!"

"You've never married."

"I've never married because I've kept a secret torch for Garrett all these years? Not that it's any of your business, but the reason I've never married is because I'm choosy. Nobody has quite yet measured up to my exacting standards."

She was definitely lying. The woman had clearly been in love with Garrett. You'd have to be blind not to see it, and even then, you'd be able to hear her adoration from the tone of her voice. Wren could understand why she'd lie. Admitting the truth could make her a suspect in Garrett's murder, making her out to be an obsessed stalker who killed him because she couldn't have him. But why did she open the coffee shop? Was it to spite him? To show him she could run a similar business just as well as he could? Or was it something else?

Why do people lie during murder investigations?

"I'm sorry for throwing a brick at you but I've already talked to the police and I have no desire to be interrogated by the local loser." Veronica patted Wren on the shoulder like you would a sick dog. "I didn't kill Garrett, and I didn't love him. Get a life."

"Maybe if you finally admit your feelings."

"You're barred from my coffee shop."

"It hasn't gone out of business yet, then?"

Veronica prepared to slap her. Wren braced for it. She could go toe to toe with this harridan all day. To be honest she was actually enjoying the verbal sparring. It made her feel alive.

"Ever since Garrett died, I've had lots of customers," said Veronica smugly. "I'm doing quite well."

"My dad dying worked out awfully well for you!" Jordan shouted.

Wren wished she could shrivel up into a ball. She felt stuck in the middle.

"How can you think I'd kill him?" Veronica asked.

"I listened to all that bull you told Wren," Jordan raged. "You more than knew Dad at high school. You were obsessed with him. When he didn't ask you to the prom you tried to kill yourself!"

"Where did you hear that?"

"Dad told me. He found you and rushed you to hospital and you grew even more obsessed with him. When he married my mom, it just killed you." Jordan walked up to her, all incandescent rage. Wren put her hand on his arm to try and calm him but he ignored her. "Don't think I didn't notice you all these years watching the house or finding ways to talk to him. You even tried to buy the house next door so you could be near him."

"That house has a south facing window."

Jordan marched over to the door and opened it. "Get out."

Veronica nodded, obviously trying to control her own anger, but for some reason she didn't let rip. She just walked away.

"I'm sorry you had to see that," said Jordan. He was staring at Veronica as she crossed the road, almost as if willing a car to run her over. "She just gets on my nerves."

"You did sabotage her business and accuse her of killing your dad," said Wren. He didn't deny the sabotage part, and her trust for him eroded just a little bit. "You can't blame her for being... crotchety?"

"That woman is too cowardly to commit murder." He looked at the door again, seeing a few customers waiting for the place to open. "Anyway, we better get to it. I need help unpacking the new coffee machine. We have customers, and I for one don't want them going to Veronica's place."

Wren suddenly wanted to go home. She hated this atmosphere. Besides, her head really was starting to hurt now. How could she stand up all day serving coffee when she felt this bad?

"I think I need to go home," Wren admitted. Her vision started to waver. "My head really hurts."

"I need you," Jordan accused. "I can't do this on my own."

"How can you expect me to..."

The world started to spin. Wren heard Jordan screaming her name before everything turned to black.

Chapter 23

"I haven't heard from you in a while."

"My husband is in jail."

"Then you need me more than ever before."

"Please leave me alone. My daughter is in hospital."

"And I'm her doctor."

Wren opened her eyes, wondering why she was in hospital. The last thing she remembered was passing out in the Metropolitan.

"What's your boyfriend doing here?" she mumbled.

Her head throbbed a little, though not as bad as it had before, and she felt slightly high. The hospital lights were too bright. It was like the sun was shining directly on her face.

"You're going to be okay," said her mom. Anthony was standing by her in his doctor's whites, looking awkward. "They thought you had a blood clot at first but it was just concussion." She smiled and took hold of Wren's hand. She felt instantly at ease. "What happened?"

"Veronica Van Clark happened," said Wren, seething. "I should press charges against that woman."

She briefly explained what had happened, during which Anthony made a swift exit. Wren felt a little sorry for him. He probably felt like the proverbial third wheel.

"She could have killed you!" Dot raged.

"I'll be fine," Wren insisted. "Don't start a feud or something. The woman's crazy."

"I'll start a feud with anyone who messes with my family."

Wren believed her. Dot was like a mother lion when someone upset someone she loved. Bullies and ex-boyfriends had often found themselves at the end of one of Dot's tongue-lashings.

"Do you remember when I was ten and Amanda Fury pushed me off my bike?" Wren asked.

Dot shrugged. "My memory is not what it used to be."

"Someone stole her bike and ran over it in their car and then threw it through her window. Was that you?"

"Ask me no questions and I shall tell you no lies."

Wren didn't know whether to be impressed or horrified. She settled on mildly pleased. A part of her was secretly glad. Her mother was not someone to be messed with.

"I went to see your father this morning," said Dot. She tried tucking in the covers on the hospital bed but Wren slapped her hand. "He wouldn't talk to me, but I could tell he was nervous. He really doesn't like prison."

"Nobody likes prison," said Wren.

Her mother sighed. "I don't understand why he would gamble like this. Is he bored with our marriage? Does he know about me and Anthony and wanted to get revenge? It doesn't make any sense."

"Had he ever had a gambling problem before?"

"We went to a few casinos every now and then. We've been to Vegas, Reno, and Atlantic City. Was he an addict all this time and I just never noticed?"

"I don't think it's anyone's fault. I think it's just something that happens."

But knowing his wife is cheating on him probably doesn't help.

"I've broken up with Anthony," Dot admitted.

"Good," said Wren. "I know he made you happy but..."

"Yes. He made me happy, but I love your father. The doctor needed to go. I need to spend all my energy on Wick now. I want our marriage to work."

It gladdened her heart to know her mother was putting her father first. She wasn't sure he deserved it, what with his recent crime spree, but if her parents could still love each other after spending ten years in jail, then they could survive this.

But what if her dad went back to jail?

She started to feel dizzy again, and soon drifted off to sleep. She dreamed about Jordan and the hatred he'd shown towards Veronica. She dreamed that he tried to murder her.

Wren awoke some time later. She tried sitting up in bed, only to find a tray with dinner on it. It was some type of meat pie with peas and a small pot of raspberry Jell-O. It looked quite nice. She tried to eat some but felt sick with every bite.

"They left you a chocolate chip cookie, but I ate it," a voice said.

It was Maureen from the unemployment office. She was sitting in a chair next to her bed reading a gossip magazine. There was a multi-colored knitted quilt on her lap. She looked like she was about to settle in to bed.

"What are you doing here?" Wren asked.

"I was visiting my mom after she had her toe removed," said Maureen, making Wren feel even sicker. "I thought I'd pop by and see you. You look like you've been in a fight with a supervillain."

"I *feel* like I've been in a fight with a supervillain."

Trust Maureen to tell her how she really looked.

"Your mother tells me you're investigating Garrett Knowles and his untimely demise." Maureen sneaked a half-eaten cookie into her mouth, chewed and swallowed quickly. "You should've come to me. I know all the local gossip."

"I've discovered some secrets during this investigation that nobody knows. I don't think you'd be any help."

Maureen grinned and pulled a small black purse from under the quilt. She took out a little notepad and a black pen.

"I notice things," said Maureen. She opened the notepad. "People avoid me because I'm odd. People treat me like I'm not there. They talk over me."

"That's not nice," said Wren. "I'm sorry."

"I'm on the spectrum, did you know that?"

Wren didn't know that, though it explained a lot. Maureen wasn't rude; she was just different.

"You listen to people talk and you write it down?" Wren asked, becoming interested. "You might be able to help me."

"I don't know much about this case. Some of the people involved are boring. This happened a month ago. I was in the park, eating breadcrumbs in front of the birds, when I overheard Katie Knowles talking on her cell phone. She was talking to some friend with a stupid name about how she'd bought life insurance for her husband worth one million dollars. She joked about how unfortunate it would be if Garrett were to die and she were to get all his money."

"That's very interesting. Why would she do that? They're already rich."

Maureen shook her head. "No, they're not. I overheard another conversation dating back six months." She searched through her thick notepad for the right page and smiled. "Garrett and Katie were arguing about her latest plastic surgery appointment. He said enough was enough and she looked perfectly fine. She said she could look so much better. He said they couldn't afford it. He said she'd spent all their money on facelifts and useless crap and bad investments and they had to be careful. She asked if they were in financial trouble. He said they were. She didn't like that."

Maybe this was about money after all, only not the kind she'd thought. What if Katie had killed her husband to get his life insurance and not the millions he had inherited from his father?

"The death was messy," said Wren. "Anything could have gone wrong. I don't think Katie would be that careless and kill him like that. She'd hire someone or make it look like suicide."

"You have to put yourself in the mind of the killer," said Maureen. "You have to think like a killer."

"This isn't *Silence of the Lambs*. I wouldn't go that far."

Maureen closed her book. "That's all I have for this case. You can thank me by buying me take out or a Netflix subscription. Goodbye."

Before Wren even had a chance to say anything Maureen had left. She couldn't help but laugh. The woman really was amazing. It was a pity she didn't have any dirt on anyone else, but Wren was starting to get the bigger picture now. As much as she hated to admit it, she was now sure Garrett was killed by a member of his own family.

Chapter 24

The couch felt like Heavenly clouds under her backside. The hospital bed had been hard as a board and she still couldn't get the smell of cabbage out of her nostrils. Why did hospitals smell of cabbage?

"I'm sorry I couldn't flit you home," said Fiona. "I really did try."

"It's okay," said Wren. "I liked the cab journey home. It gave me time to think."

"The scenery around here is very lovely."

She hadn't noticed. The murder was constant and foremost on her mind now. She knew she was nearly there. It was either Katie or Jordan, but without any proof there was nothing she could do.

"How do you feel?" Fiona asked, sitting down beside her. The two cats were asleep on the armchair, ignorant of their master's return. "You still look woozy."

"I'm actually fine," Wren admitted. "The night in the hospital did me wonders. I have a little headache but nothing to worry about."

She suddenly remembered Sheriff Fisher and her suspicion that he might be Jordan's father, and Aarna's claim that Garrett's death her was her own fault, and all her theories went out the window. Maybe she wasn't as close to finding the killer as she'd thought.

"It's all so hopeless," she wailed.

"It's not that bad," said Fiona. "The brick didn't do any damage."

"I meant the murder. I thought I was about to figure out who did it, but I forgot some things, and now I'm just as confused as ever."

"Maybe you should leave this to the police for now, until you feel better."

"Dad is counting on me."

"He's not even being charged with Garrett's murder. I know we've had...I suppose you could call it fun, but it's over. You're injured. Leave it be."

Maybe Fiona was right. This had nothing to do with her. The sheriff didn't think her father killed Garrett, but as far as she was aware, they weren't even looking for another suspect. Should she just give it up?

There was a twinge of pain in her head. It was like someone had stuck a knitting needle between her ears.

"Are you still in pain?" Fiona asked.

"A little," Wren lied.

Fiona nodded and placed her hands on Wren's head. She laughed, wondering what was going on, but there was such an intense look of concentration on the angel's face that she let her be. Something wondrous was happening, she could feel it.

The pain shifted. It didn't leave entirely, but it was a mere ache now, something she could live with.

"What did you do?" Wren asked.

"I healed you," said Fiona proudly. "At least I think I did. This is the first time I've done something like this, and like I've said before, I'm only a trainee, so I don't have much power, but I think I healed you."

"You did. A bit."

"Oh."

Wren smiled and pulled the angel into a hug.

"You made me feel better," said Wren, grinning uncontrollably. "You didn't get rid of the pain entirely, but you did it. You really healed me."

"Are you sure?" Fiona asked, her confidence still wavering. "You aren't just humoring me or anything are you?"

"What you did was amazing. Thank you so much."

Fiona started to cry, and Wren pulled her in for another hug. She needed it. They both needed it.

"That was really the first time you tried to heal someone?" Wren asked.

The angel wiped at her eyes. "Juniper and Brock told me it was very difficult to do, even for experienced angels, but I had to do something. I don't like seeing people in pain. It's the nurse in me."

"So, you used to be a nurse. That explains a lot."

"I shouldn't have told you that. Forget I said anything."

The cats were sitting up, staring at Fiona in what Wren could only describe as abject wonder. She'd never seen her Gracie do anything like that before. It was as if she'd seen something that awed her. Could a cat even understand what had happened, or had they just picked up on the energy in the room?

There was a copy of *The Snowflake Bay Herald* on the coffee table. The front page caught her eye. She grabbed the paper and started to read.

"Have you seen this?" Wren demanded.

Fiona said, "I brought the paper in this morning. I didn't look at it. I had to come and fetch you from the hospital."

The article said her father had confessed to murder. He had been officially charged with killing Garrett.

Chapter 25

"What the hell are you playing at?" Wren raged.

She's stormed over to the police station in such a fury that she ignored every person she passed. Even Fiona's voice of reason, begging her to calm down, went through one ear and out the other. All she could focus on was her father and how she was going to scream at the sheriff for betraying them.

The sheriff said, "Let me tell you and..."

"You said you didn't think he did it!" Wren shouted. The other deputies were looking at the floor, probably wishing they were anywhere but here. Keegan was standing by his father, trying to save face, but he too looked embarrassed. "You said that..."

"He told me he wanted to talk, and he confessed," said the sheriff. "I had to charge him with murder."

"He'd never confess. He didn't do it."

"There's nothing I can do. He admitted to it."

Wren sat down, feeling unsteady. It didn't make any sense. Her father was innocent. He could never murder anybody!

"It's true," said Keegan. His voice was low, compassionate. He kneeled down in front of her. "He said that Garrett came out of the back room while he robbing the till and he punched him. When Garrett was knocked out he pushed the coffee machine onto his head to kill him."

"You know he didn't do it," said Wren. She felt true despair. "You know it."

"I know that, but we have to take him at his word."

"Let me talk to him."

"He doesn't want to see anybody."

She glared daggers at Keegan and said, "Take me to my father now or I will make a scene that will make my last one look like a Bible study class."

Keegan nodded, and he led her towards the cell. Everyone else stayed behind.

"Dad?" she called.

He was standing in his cell, staring at her. He looked like a man who had lost everything. He was a shell.

"Why did you admit to it?" she demanded, saving her last reserves of anger and betrayal for her father. "Why?"

"I killed Garrett," Wick stated.

"Did someone threaten you? Is someone making you do this?"

"You have to face the fact that I'm a murderer. I'm not proud of what I did, but I had to do it."

"I don't believe you."

He laughed bitterly and said, "You have to believe me because it's true."

Wren wouldn't put up with this. Someone had gotten to him. Maybe he'd heard about the message on her door and the person watching her house and wanted to protect her? There had to something he wasn't telling her. She'd never believe he was a murderer. Never.

Only Fiona and I know about the graffiti and the spying. I never even told Mom or Keegan.

Her father would only worry further if she insisted on proving him innocent. It was time to try out her acting chops.

"You really killed him," she said.

He nodded. "I'm sorry."

"Then maybe prison is the best place for you."

She turned her back on him and walked away. It was the hardest thing she'd ever had to do in her life.

FIONA FELT LIKE SHE had an extra arm. Sheriff Fisher and the other deputies kept staring at her. They were probably wondering who she was and why she was with Wren.

"Who are you?" Sheriff Fisher asked. He looked at her oddly, as if she was utterly fascinating. "I've never seen you around town before."

"I'm a friend of Wren," said the angel. "Fiona McDonald. I was here the other day with Wren."

He studied her for a few moments. "I know you, though, right? I'm sure I do. Little Fiona..."

Fiona felt awkward again. The same thing was happening with the sheriff as what happened with his son. His brain was somehow creating false memories to make her fit into his life. What was going on?

The sheriff shook his head and smiled. "Glad to see you back in town. It's been too long. How are your parents?"

Parents?

"They've retired to Jersey," said Fiona. "The island, not the state."

She had no idea why she said that. It must be because she watched a documentary on *Discovery* last night about the Nazi occupation of Jersey. During her time in London she'd actually met a British officer whose family were trapped on the island. He'd been worried sick about them. She'd always wondered what happened to him.

"I'm glad you're here for Wren," said the sheriff. "This is going to be a hard time for her. I was as surprised as she was when Wick confessed, but I had to take his word for it. If he really did it then he should pay."

There was unexpected venom and emotion in his voice.

"Did anybody visit him in the past day?" Fiona asked. "Maybe someone threatened him."

"He had no visitors other than his wife and Reba."

She told him about the graffiti and the person watching the house.

"You think someone got to him?" said the sheriff.

"I do," Wren announced, walking up to them. Fiona could feel her simmering anger. It was palpable. "That man is not a murderer and we all know it."

"But how could someone threaten him?" Keegan asked, trying to play devil's advocate. "Only Reba and Dot came to see him. Are you saying either your mom or your cousin killed Garrett and threatened your dad?"

"No, said Wren. She turned to Sheriff Fisher and pointed at him. "I think *you* threatened him. I think you killed Garrett."

Chapter 26

To say Wren regretted her words the moment they came out of her mouth was an understatement, but it was too late now. The cat was out of the bag. She only hoped her friendship with Keegan could survive this.

"Do you want to leave before you make a bigger fool of yourself?" the sheriff asked calmly. She was at least thankful for that. "Think about this."

"I think you found out that Jordan was your son, and you confronted Garrett about it," Wren accused. "When he told you the story Katie had told him you killed him in an angry rage."

Time seemed to stop in the police station. Every deputy turned to look at her. Deputy Stark even dropped the cream eclair he was eating. Fiona bit her lip. Keegan looked from Wren to his father and back again, seeming so totally gob smacked he couldn't speak.

"You think Jordan is my son?" asked the sheriff.

The center of attention was not an easy place to be. Wren wanted the world to crumble around her.

I've gone and done it now...

"Wren?" Keegan asked. "What do you know?"

She looked at him, and then back towards his father. "I'm sorry. I never should have said anything. Forget I ever brought it up."

"This is not something I'm ever likely to forget," said the sheriff bitterly. Now he *was* angry. "Explain yourself before I think up some reason to arrest you."

"I'm listening too," Keegan added, looking at her like he didn't know her any more. "Wren?"

"I noticed when I found you watching Katie's house that you were in love with her. Katie claimed she had a one-night stand with someone but was so drunk she couldn't remember who it was. I thought she was lying. The only person who could've gotten to Dad to blackmail him was someone in this station. I put two and two together. Sheriff Fisher is Jordan's father. He killed Garrett. He threatened my father to make him confess to the murder."

"What proof do you have?" demanded the sheriff.

"None. Just my gut."

The sheriff ordered everyone out. The deputies, including Fiona as well, made a swift exit. Wren felt cornered. She wished she could take it back but it was too late. She had to suffer the consequences of her actions.

"Sit down," the sheriff ordered. His tone was firm. "Both of you."

"Is Jordan my brother?" Keegan asked.

"Does Jordan look black to you?" his father asked him.

"He is quite tanned. I always thought he used tanning booths or something but..."

The sheriff walked up to his son and put his hands on his shoulders. Wren waited patiently for her turn.

"Jordan is not my son," the sheriff stated.

"Did you have an affair with Katie?" Keegan asked. He was staring at his father like he was a stranger, and it tore Wren apart. She'd caused this. "Is that why Mom left?"

Keegan's mother had left the family when he was a toddler. They hadn't seen her since. Growing up without a mother had been hard on him.

"Your mom left because she couldn't cope as a mother," said the sheriff. "I have never slept with Katie. I never would sleep with Katie. Your mother was the first and last woman I ever slept with." The sheriff took a deep breath. "Son...I'm gay."

This was the last thing Wren was expecting. Keegan appeared too deep in shock to even reply.

"Did you hear what I said?" the sheriff asked.

Keegan nodded. "How long have you known? Why didn't you tell me when I came out?"

"I'm the master of denial. I only admitted it to myself when someone I'd loved for a long time kissed me and told me they loved me."

"You weren't in love with Katie," said Wren. The truth was obvious now she really thought about it. "You were in love with her husband. You were in love with Garrett."

Sheriff Fisher sat down on the edge of his desk. He was crying. Wren pulled a *Kleenex* out of her pocket and passed it to him. He smiled.

"Were you and Garrett seeing each other?" Wren asked.

"For nearly two years," the sheriff admitted. He laughed, almost like the burden of revealing the truth healed him. "We'd finally gotten to the stage where we wanted it all out in the open. We were sick of lying and sneaking around when all we wanted was to be together. So, we planned to bring all the family together and tell them at the same time. We knew it was going to be hard but we had to do it. We couldn't live a lie any longer."

"The dinner party you had planned for the weekend after Garrett died," said Garrett. "I thought that was Katie's idea."

"It was," said the sheriff. "But Garrett and I were going to hijack it with our announcement."

Rob and Garrett been so close to getting their happy ever after. No wonder Garrett had seemed so ecstatic when he talked about it, even with a bleeding nose.

Life is so unfair.

"I'm so sorry you had to go through this alone," said Keegan.

Father and son hugged, but all Wren could think about now was Katie. Now she had even more of a reason to want her husband dead.

"Did Katie know about you and Garrett?" Wren asked him.

"You know Katie," said the sheriff. He wiped at his eyes. "If she knew she'd make a scene about it. That woman revels in drama."

"You shouldn't be worried about her. She took out a secret life insurance policy on Garrett worth a million dollars. They were almost bankrupt. If that isn't reason alone to want him dead, then knowing her husband is gay and about to divorce her surely will."

It all made sense. It all fitted together!

"How do you know all this?" Sheriff Fisher asked.

"I'm better at detective work than even I imagined," Wren revealed enigmatically.

She refused to give away her sources. Maureen could be critical if this went to court. Plus, she didn't want the killer, if indeed it was Katie, to find out. There might be another murder otherwise.

"Are you absolutely sure she didn't know?" Keegan asked. He was looking worried now. "This is important."

The sheriff said, "I honestly don't know. We were careful."

Wren thought back to her conversations with Katie, picking apart every last word. There had to be a clue in there.

Then it hit her. "She did say something derogatory about his favorite color being lavender. Wasn't that a thing in the fifties related to communism or something?"

The sheriff nodded. "The government persecuted homosexuals, saying they were a threat to national security. It was called the 'Lavender Scare.' Garrett and I talked about it once at the Metropolitan, late at night."

Wren grimaced. It was like something out of Nazi Germany. How could her own country do something so awful?

"Maybe Katie turned up to see Garrett and overheard it," Keegan suggested.

"You really think she killed Garrett?" the sheriff asked.

"If her husband dies, she gets a million dollars." Wren started to pace, putting it all together. It made more sense than the sheriff being the killer. "If Garrett divorces her, she gets virtually nothing because the family are almost broke. I think she did it, but it's up to you, Sheriff."

He nodded. "Let's go and arrest her."

THEY FOUND KATIE FACE down, floating on the surface of her pool. She was dead.

Chapter 27

"I *killed my husband.*

We were almost out of money. I loved my lifestyle and I was afraid of losing that. When you grow up with nothing, you learn to cling on to what you have with everything in your power.

I thought I could kill my husband and cash in his life insurance check without consequences, but I felt remorse. Deep remorse. It wasn't until Garrett was actually dead that I realized how much I loved him and couldn't live without him. I'd made a grave mistake.

Tell my son I love him.

Love, Katie"

They'd found the note on a lounger at the side of the pool. It was written on a piece of expensive paper. There was a silver pen resting by it, Katie's name written on its side.

"It doesn't mention Garrett leaving her for me," said the sheriff, rereading the note again through a plastic evidence bag. "So she didn't know after all."

Wren shook her head. "No. She knew." She thought back to that conversation again, really thinking about the expression on Katie's face as she said the word 'lavender.' "She definitely knew. I know it in my gut."

"Then you would've thought that she'd use her suicide note to vent about it," said Keegan. "She wasn't the type to keep quiet when she could cause a scene."

"This isn't suicide," said Wren. "Someone murdered her and made it look like suicide." The sheriff seemed unduly upset. "Did you see anybody come to her house? You were still keeping an eye on her, right?"

"I didn't watch her last night. I thought she was safe. I... I went home. I didn't think she was in any danger. Maybe if I stayed I could have saved her."

"If it's any consolation I doubt you would've seen anything. This is a really big house. The murderer might have come over the back fence." She looked around, seeing a large tree out the back. "They could've climbed up that tree. There's any number of ways they could've sneaked past you."

He didn't appear to be assuaged, but there was nothing she could do about that.

"If someone was that desperate to kill Katie they might have killed you too," said Wren.

"They could've tried," said the sheriff. "I would've shot them."

She studied the body as it was dragged out of the pool by the deputies. They were wet and miserable and looked like they wished they were anywhere else. Katie's body was wrinkled and grey. Wren felt sorry for her.

"Are you okay?" Wren asked.

Deputy Stark nodded. "It's too much."

She knew how he felt. She'd gone her whole life without seeing a dead body and now she'd seen two in a week.

"Maybe she didn't mention Dad and Garrett's affair in the note because she knew Jordan might read it?" Keegan suggested. Wren nodded, agreeing with him. "She perhaps didn't want him to know."

"I wanted him to know," said the sheriff. "He needed to know who his father really was."

"Did Katie know this?" Keegan asked.

The sheriff sighed sadly. "Perhaps not. Maybe this was suicide after all. We probably won't know for sure until we do an autopsy, and even then, we probably won't be able to tell whether it was suicide or not."

"It wasn't suicide," said Wren again. "Katie was a brash, waspish woman. She would never kill herself, not in a million years."

Keegan and his father both nodded, agreeing with her.

Maybe there's something I can do now while waiting for the autopsy results.

"I think I'm going to be sick," said Wren, covering her mouth. "I'm just going to find the bathroom. I don't want to contaminate the crime scene."

She quickly fled, wishing she didn't have to lie, but she needed to have a snoop. The police had their ways, and she had her own.

I need to find an example of Katie's handwriting.

She entered the house, still finding herself astonished by its opulence. It was pretty obvious now why the family was broke. Katie had decorated the place like some sort of gauche royal palace. It was elegant but tacky as well.

Wren crept up the stairs, looking for Katie's bedroom. The upstairs was even more lavish. She lost count of the numbers of antique cabinets with vases and sculptures. There was a bookshelf filled with self-help books and several more portraits of Katie, all done in different styles from watercolor to Picasso. Some of them were actually quite stunning.

"What are you doing?" Fiona asked, poking her head from out of a room.

Wren rolled her eyes. "Snooping. How do you know where to find me? Have you got me tagged like a cat or something?"

"I always know where to find you. It's just an angel thing."

She followed Fiona into what Wren could only describe as a rich person's mountain cabin. There was a faux polar bear rug on the floor (she hoped it was fake). It reminded her of the hotel she'd stayed in when visiting Switzerland. It was homely and warm and inviting, but posher and more obnoxious.

"I'll assume this is Katie's bedroom," said Wren.

She headed over to the bed, which had a thick wooden frame. There was a luxurious woolen blanket draped over it. There was a small bedside table. One of the drawers was slightly open. She had a peek inside.

"Look at this," Wren called, pulling out a small notebook. She opened it and started to read. "This is odd."

"What is it?" Fiona asked.

"Katie is writing a novel." She sat on the bed and continued to read. "It seems to be about a poor orphan girl who marries a boring man with flatulence problems and then dumps him for a sexy millionaire and..." Wren cringed. "And it's very filthy. I didn't even know that position was possible without breaking both your legs." She read a bit more, enjoying it. It was pure, unadulterated filth. "There's a bit of Katie in here, and the millionaire sounds like Garrett. I think it may be partly autobiographical."

She closed the book and put it back where she'd found it. The handwriting seemed to match the one from the suicide note, though maybe only an expert could detect any noticeable differences.

"Writing a novel seems like a big task," commented Fiona, examining a silver candlestick on a sideboard. "I'm not sure I'd have the patience."

Wren opened some more drawers, finding marriage certificates, birth certificates, and notebooks. There was writing in each of them. Mostly it was ideas or character profiles, but a lot of it was prose. It was good prose, even though half of it was explicit love scenes. Katie was a decent writer. There was a letter in the bottom drawer. It was from a publisher.

"Hey," said Wren, skimming through the letter. "This says that Katie sold her book to a publisher. They were going to give her an advance of a million dollars to publish it." She grinned, impressed. "People will pay for filth." She pulled out another letter, which was even more explosive than the first. "She's sold the movie rights for five million. Katie was going to be set up for life. She didn't need to bump off her husband for the money."

"Maybe she just did it out of spite," said Fiona. "Her husband was going to leave her for his best friend."

Fiona was right. This didn't prove one way or another that Katie was innocent. All it proved was that Katie didn't need to murder Garrett for the life insurance. She could've killed him as revenge for planning to leave her. But if that was true then why would she not mention it in the suicide note?

"I'm confused," Wren admitted. Half of her was desperate to read more of Katie's erotic fiction. "This is giving me a headache."

"Do you really, truly think my mother didn't kill herself?" Jordan asked.

He was standing in the doorway, watching them. She'd been too engrossed in her own thinking to even notice he was there. He looked devastated. The poor man had lost both parents in a matter of days.

"I'm not sure," said Wren. She thought for a moment but stayed true to her path. "Yes. I'm sure she didn't kill herself, and I'm sure she didn't kill your father."

Jordan said, "I know you can find out who did this. I trust you."

He walked in and kissed her. She felt lightheaded for a moment but didn't tell him to stop. It was electric.

"Come over tonight," he offered. "I don't think I can be on my own."

"I'd be glad to," said Wren.

He kissed her again and walked away. Wren almost passed out.

"Stop being so pathetic," Fiona hissed. "He just manipulated you. Pretty soon he'll have you making his bed for him."

"I'm not an idiot," said Wren. "I do know that."

She sat back on the bed. Of course, she knew Jordan was manipulating her. She just didn't care. She was going to further investigate his father's death anyway. She might as well get something out of it.

"Anyway," said Wren, standing up. She had work to do. "I need to talk to Aarna."

"Have you considered the possibility that Jordan killed his parents?" asked Fiona.

"Of course, I have," said Wren. "Which is why I'm not going to come and see him tonight. I'd be an idiot to spend time alone with him."

"Yes. Of course."

Have I been too blinded by Jordan's grief and sexual charisma to remember he was a suspect too?

AARNA GUPTA LIVED IN a small apartment over the thrift store on Abraham Lincoln Avenue. The windows had colorful red and purple curtains. The girl's parents owned a fabric store on Main Street. Wren had shopped there on occasion.

Her door was half open.

"Something is wrong," Wren whispered.

Fiona clutched her hand. "Has the killer gotten to Aarna too?"

She pushed the door open and they stepped quietly inside. Aarna was lying prostrate on the floor. She didn't appear to be moving.

Chapter 28

Wren tried not to panic as she ran up to Aarna. She took her pulse first, which showed a heartbeat. She turned the girl over and noticed dried vomit all over her purple top. She stunk like booze.

"She's drunk," Wren stated.

Fiona grinned impishly. "I know just the cure for that. Wait a moment."

The angel walked into the kitchen and found a brown mixing bowl. She filled it with cold water from the faucet, walked over to the passed out Aarna, and chucked the liquid all over her.

"What's going on?" Aarna screamed, jumping up.

"We'd like to talk."

Half an hour later Aarna was looking a little more refreshed. Fiona had made something in the kitchen that seemed to instantly cure her hangover. She didn't say what she put in it, but did state she used to make it regularly for her father. Wren didn't like to press the matter. It seemed like a sensitive subject.

"How are you doing?" Wren asked.

"You should've just left me," Aarna muttered miserably.

"Where were you the night Garrett died?" Fiona shouted out.

Wren gave her friend a cautious look. "Perhaps now is not the time to be flinging around accusations. You know how that went with Sheriff Fisher."

"You accusing Sheriff Fisher of murder helped him to come out to his son and made him a better person. He had a catharsis because of you."

Wren never thought of it like that. Sheriff Fisher did seem a little less burdened after telling his son the truth. Perhaps her callously accusing him of cold-blooded murder in a public place had been worth it?

"Do you think I killed Garrett?" Aarna asked.

"You did tell me you thought it was your fault that he died," said Wren.

"That's because it me who started all this off in the first place." Aarna rubbed her arm anxiously. "I was the one who bought Jordan that DNA ancestry kit. I only did it for a laugh! I didn't expect it to turn out like this."

"I don't understand."

"Jordan killed him, didn't he? He was so angry when he found out Garrett wasn't his father. I'd never seen him like that before. It scared me. We'd always been such good friends. You know we dated in high school?" She smiled dreamily. "That boy could do things with his hands..."

Wren smiled too. Jordan really was wonderful.

"Why did you break up if he was so wonderful?" Fiona asked.

"He cheated on me." She looked uncomfortable for a moment. "But it was okay. I got over it. Like I said, we became friends." The woman was lying. Nobody got over being cheated on, and it was obvious by the look on her face. It still hurt her even now.

"You really think Jordan killed his father?" Wren asked.

"Like I said, he was angry," said Aarna. "I honestly thought he had killed him when I found out Garrett was dead."

"But what about now?"

She shrugged. "I honestly don't know. Maybe."

Fiona went to brew some black coffee using a Mr. Coffee machine. The bitter liquid made them all feel a little better.

"Where were you at the time of the murder?" Wren asked.

Aarna pierced them with a withering gaze. "We're back to that, are we? I had no motive to want Garrett dead. He was good to me. He gave me a job."

"Humor me."

"I was at home with my parents if you must know." She looked embarrassed. "I was begging them for money, okay? I owed Garrett a lot for that job, but I was sick of it. I'm not meant to do such menial work, you know? I have my own YouTube channel!" Fiona looked to Wren, confused. The angel had no idea what the woman was talking about. "My parents have money. I thought the least they could do was give me some of it. After they said no and accused me of being spoiled, I stayed for dinner. They were having a rare evening when they weren't fighting." She shivered. "I hate it when they fight."

Wren believed her. For someone like Aarna admitting to spending the evening with her parents was social suicide.

I wonder what she does on her YouTube channel? It's probably something lame like opening boxes or something.

Aarna was tapping on her cell phone, ignoring them already. Wren felt like smacking her across the face for being so ignorant. She still looked shaken, but not nearly as much as she had been.

"So, what do you do on your YouTube channel?" Wren asked.

Aarna grinned smugly. "I order stuff from Amazon and open the boxes and film them. My fans love it. One day I'm going to be more famous than PewDiePie."

Wren nodded, trying not to laugh. How predictable.

And who the hell is PewDiePie?

"Am I still under suspicion?" Aarna asked. "I'm not a murderer."

"Five minutes ago, you were in pieces," Fiona stated.

"There's nothing I can do about people being murdered." She put down her cell and stared Wren in the eye. "I see the way you're looking at me, judging me. I'm not just a typical, stupid American whose hands are fixed to her cell phone. If I even think about Garrett being killed in such a horrible way for too long I'm going to go mad. I can't be like that again. I can't be... the type of person who breaks down over everything. If I do that. I'll end up back at the point I was when my brother died. I was so depressed that I couldn't even eat." She walked into the kitchen and brought in a large Amazon box. "This is my therapy. It keeps me sane and people, for some weird reason, like to watch me doing it. It makes me happy."

Wren felt like the worst person in the world. She had judged Aarna too harshly, thinking her some flighty socialite. She had to make amends.

"Perhaps I could appear in one of your videos?" Wren offered. "You could use my house."

Aarna smiled. "You have that big house on Grantchester Street, right? That place is wicked."

"We'll set it up some time." Wren paused and added, "I'm sorry for being a cow."

"You're forgiven."

They left Aarna to it. When they got outside it was already going dark. Wren realized she'd been non-stop all day and she hadn't thought about eating or taking a rest once. She needed a break. Garrett and Katie's killer could wait until tomorrow. It wasn't as if they were going anywhere.

"Let's go home and order take out," Wren suggested.

"Good idea," said Fiona, excited. "I'd love to try Chinese food. It wasn't really a thing back when I was alive."

"All the clues about you are slowly building up. One day I'll piece it all together."

"Good luck with that."

Chapter 29

Something nagged at Wren's memory all night. She would sleep for a while, haunted by dreams of Katie floating in the pool, and then wake up. She'd seen something in Katie's house that had passed her by but was sure was an important clue, something that would unlock the mystery. What was it? Why couldn't she remember?

The two cats were sitting on the edge of her bed, staring at her in annoyance. There was no look more terrifying than that of a cat which had been rudely awoken in the middle of the night.

"What do you two think?" she asked them.

Gracie meowed. Casper kept silent.

"You want me to meditate?" she asked them. "You know I can't do that. My brain is always too busy." She laughed. "Fine. I'll try it."

Ten minutes later she gave up. She could hear the cats breathing and it annoyed her. Meditation was for people who had far more patience.

"Are you okay?" Fiona asked.

She had flitted into her bedroom. Fiona was wearing red and white striped tartan pajamas. They looked cute on her.

"I thought I had an epiphany, but I was wrong," Wren admitted.

"Have you tried meditating?" said Fiona.

Wren rolled her eyes. "Go back to bed. I want to try and get some sleep."

"I thought you might be sad because of... well, you know."

"I honestly don't know."

"It's yours and Alex's wedding anniversary today. I saw it on that hunky firefighters and their cats' calendar you have in the kitchen." Fiona blushed. "Mr. March really is quite a man, hmm?"

The date had totally passed her by. She'd been so busy with the murders and her dad's arrest. How could she forget? She normally spent her wedding anniversary sitting on the porch and feeling sorry for herself, drunk on apple cider and a stomach full of chocolate truffles. She usually spent the week leading up to the day in a state of either dread or deep depression. Did this mean she was finally over it?

"What are you thinking?" Fiona asked.

"I honestly forgot all about it."

"Maybe that's a good thing. Maybe you're finally ready to move on."

"I don't know. Maybe. Probably."

Then it hit her – the marriage certificates in Katie's drawer. She'd only glossed over them really in her search for something more interesting, but she'd seen the names of the people she'd married on them.

Katie said her first husband was boring, a little obsessive.

She saw him on the night Jordan was conceived. She claimed she saw him leave, but what if he didn't leave? What if he came back?

Jordan's troubling DNA results...

The man in Katie's novel, her first husband, with the flatulence problem...

All the other little things which she'd observed but ignored rolled back into her head. They made a startling, but scary, picture.

"I know who did it," said Wren.

Now all she had to do was exact some sort of plan. She didn't want to end up as victim number three.

Chapter 30

"I never suspected you," Wren admitted, keeping her distance. "Not once."

"I don't understand," they said.

"You were never on my radar. You didn't appear to have a personal connection to any of the victims, but I was wrong."

They walked out onto the porch. She took a deep breath. This was going to be hard, but she had to do it.

"Why are you looking at me like I'm a murderer?" they asked.

"That's because you are a murderer," Wren stated. "You knocked Garrett to the floor and pushed a coffee machine on his head. You threatened to have me killed if my father didn't confess to killing Garrett. You drugged Katie and threw her in her own swimming pool to drown her and frame her instead, for what reason I don't know. You put threatening graffiti on my door. You spied on me. You're a monster."

"This is ridiculous," said Cedric. "Why would I do any of this?"

Wren was starting to feel more confident now. She had yet to rattle him, or even get an emotion out of him, but she wasn't finished yet. Far from it.

"How long have you known that you were Jordan's father?" she asked.

"I am not Jordan's father," Cedric stated.

"You and Katie grew up together in the orphanage, right?" Wren shook her head. "No. You have a brother."

"Our parents died when Jackson and I were both fifteen. We were twins. He was fostered but I wasn't because I was deemed to have issues." He didn't elaborate, and so Wren had to assume it meant he was a psycho back then, too. "I ended up in the orphanage with Katie. After I turned eighteen, just after Katie, my brother and I got an apartment together in Snowflake Bay."

Wren nodded. That made sense. Everyone knew about the famous lawyer Jackson Roper, Snowflake Bay's golden boy. Cedric had seemingly soared so far under the radar she didn't recognize the name when she agreed to out with him.

"So, Katie married you so she could escape the orphanage and try and have a normal life." Wren took a deep breath. It was time to needle a confession out of him. "But you're just creepy and boring. She knew she'd made a mistake and so she dumped you."

Cedric bared his teeth as he said, "She didn't know what she had."

"Then one night, years later, you saw her in a nightclub. She was so drunk she didn't know what she was doing. You seduced her and after a fumble in the bathroom she got pregnant with Jordan. Some would call that rape. She was drunk. She had no idea what she was doing."

"That's garbage."

"Jordan has the FAP gene, just like you." Cedric appeared shocked. He obviously didn't know this. "I looked it up online. FAP can lead to several illnesses, including colon cancer. You had colon cancer, which is why you wear a colostomy bag. You made the mistake of confiding in one of the drag queens at 'The Good, the Bad, and the Fabulous'. This condition is quite rare. It didn't take a genius to realize you're Jordan's father."

He sighed and put a hand to his stomach. There was a slight bulge there. He was touching his colostomy bag.

He kept touching it during our date!

"I have to wear this thing for the rest of my life," he said sadly. "You have no idea what it's like."

"My heart bleeds for you," said Wren, though a part of her did feel for him. Nobody deserved cancer.

"Jordan has to get a colonoscopy," said Cedric. "I don't want him to have to suffer through this."

"So, you admit it. You're his father."

He nodded. "I found out when..."

"Let me. You heard Jordan and Garrett arguing while you were in the Metropolitan bathroom."

"The walls are thin in those back rooms."

"I still don't get why you killed Garrett." She thought about it some more and came up with a hypothesis. "You went to talk to him and tell him you were Jordan's father. He laughed it off. You told him about yourself and Katie in the club bathroom and he got angry. He probably called you a rapist or something." Cedric flinched, his lip quivering in barely concealed anger. "He attacked you, and you pushed him. You saw the coffee machine and decided to end his life right there and then to stop him from telling Katie what you did."

"Katie is still the love of my life."

For some reason that irked Wren. Why was he still pursuing her if he was still in love with Katie? Was she just some sort of poor second prize?

"Then why did you kill her?" Wren asked. "If you'd let her be, then my father would've been charged with Garrett's murder and you would've gotten away with it. Oh, and thank you for that. I assume you pretended to be Jackson and talked to him and threatened to have me killed if he didn't confess."

"She wouldn't love me!" Cedric raged, ignoring the theory about her father. It was like he didn't even matter. It made her furious. "Even though her husband was dead, and I told her I was Jordan's father and we could be a proper family together, she still wouldn't love me! She was so selfish. I was the one she needed. I was the one she should love. Do you know she laughed at me? She said I was crazy and that she could never love a boring, deluded pervert like me." He was crying now. Wren started to realize she'd bitten more than she could chew. Cedric really was raving. "She said she never loved me. She said she only used me to create a life for herself. So, I decided to kill her. I popped some sleeping pills into her wine, waited for her to fall asleep, and I picked her up and threw her into the pool. It was easier than I imagined. She looked so peaceful."

Wren felt ill. "You murdered the woman you professed to love."

"I'll always love her." He smiled creepily and turned the full force of his gaze onto Wren. She cringed a little. "But I was starting to have feelings for you, too. Why do you think I warned you to stay away from investigating the murder? I didn't want you to find out it was me. I wanted to play the long game, with dates and meetings, so you'd fall in love with me gradually. It was working, right?"

"Not really. No. You disgust me."

"You know what I do to people who abuse me."

He pulled a gun out of his belt. He pointed it at her. Time seemed to slow down. She knew she could do this. Cedric wasn't a fit man.

She could take him. Her taekwondo training was finally going to be useful at long last.

"You know too much," he said. "I have to kill you now."

"People know I'm here."

She felt her muscles tense for the fight to come. She itched to punch him.

"Do they?" he asked.

She threw her left fist out. He ducked.

"Useless!" Cedric shouted.

The gun seemed to be closer now. She could almost see down the length of its barrel.

"What was that supposed to be?" Cedric demanded.

She kicked him in the stomach and tried to grab the gun. He was about to smash her in the head with his weapon when she pulled back.

This is doing no good!

A shot fired out from across the street. Sheriff Fisher and Keegan emerged from their hiding places behind a parked car.

"I've recorded everything," said Wren.

"Then I've got nothing to lose," spat Cedric.

He fired the gun.

Chapter 31

"Hello Wren."

She was standing on a bridge overlooking a small river. Multicolored dolphins splashed about in the waters. She appeared to be in New York City, but instead of roads there were canals. It was stunning.

"Where am I?" Wren asked. She shielded her eyes as she looked at the sun. "What happened?"

Fiona smiled and said, "You're in Golden, a city in Heaven. This is where I live. It's beautiful, right?"

The events of her confrontation with Cedric came back to her like a lightning bolt. It almost made her fall over the side of the bridge.

"He shot me!" Wren exclaimed. "Oh no! I'm dead!"

"You're not dead," said Fiona, slightly amused. "The bullet grazed your left arm. It's a good job Cedric didn't go to a target practice."

"Why am I here if I'm not dead? Not that I'm complaining. This place really is stunning."

"After you got shot, I thought I was a failure and I requested from Juniper that I be transferred to someone else. She wouldn't have it. She insisted I stick by you to the bitter end."

"My life is not that bad. Well, maybe it is."

An angel in a business suit walked by. He appeared to be a Neanderthal man. Wren couldn't help but stare.

"So she told me I could tell you who I really am," said Fiona.

Wren smiled. "Oh, I already know that – Great-Grandmother."

"I can't say that I'm not surprised you figured it out."

"You're my great-grandmother, on my father's side. It was easy to work out really, mainly because of all the little clues you kept revealing matched up with stories I'd heard from Grandpa when I was little about the nurse who defied her family and went to England to help during the Second World War. You left behind a husband and a small baby son called Harold."

"That was the hardest thing I ever had to do, but I felt a calling. People needed me."

"Grandpa understood. Even though he couldn't remember you, he knew how brave and selfless you were. He was so proud. I'm so proud."

"I know he had a mostly good life. I know you've all had mostly good lives. I watched from up here. It just would've nice to be there."

Wren looked up with wonder as a flock of angels flew by. Fiona laughed.

"Are you leaving?" Wren asked. "Is this a goodbye?"

Fiona shook her head. "Your life is still a complete train wreck. I doubt you'll be getting rid of me any time soon."

"My life is not a train wreck, merely a ... derailment."

"See! You're already getting a little bit more optimistic, and that was after two murders and someone shooting you. We could win this yet."

They watched as a simple wooden boat floated under the bridge. In it were two angels, a man and a woman, holding hands. Their wing feathers were golden. They looked up at them and waved.

"Can we stay here a while longer?" Wren asked. She felt so content. "I don't want to go back yet."

"Of course!" Fiona was giddy with excitement. She grabbed her hands. "Let me take you to see Brock. We can have lunch at my favorite burger place, and then we can go to David Bowie's club and watch him play and..."

WREN OPENED HER EYES. She was in hospital. She was fairly sure it was the same bed she ended up in when Veronica threw that brick at her.

Damn it! I didn't want to leave!

"Wrenny!" Dot screamed. "Oh, you're awake!"

Wren groaned. "What happened? Where's Cedric?"

"Don't you worry about him. Just try and get better."

"Tell me what happened to Cedric."

"He tried to shoot you again after you went down. Sheriff Fisher shot him, and he fell into a coma. They don't think he's ever going to come out of it."

A little part of her felt sorry for him. Only a little part. He'd only wanted to be loved. In the end that desperation had sent him down a dangerous path of obsession and murder. Now he was going to spend the rest of his life in a coma. Was it a fitting end, or just simply sad?

"I think it's safe to say that Cedric was the latest in a long line of dating disasters," Wren muttered. "I think I'll become a nun."

"You really don't have any luck, do you?" Her mum gave her a kiss on the cheek. "There's someone out there for you. I just know it. You have to be patient. They may come now, or next week, or when you're my age, but I know they'll come."

Wren didn't believe her. Her love life had to be cursed. There was no other explanation for how calamitous it was. For the time being she wanted to concentrate on getting well. After that? She had no idea. She was sure Fiona would help her.

THE MURDERER LOOKED like he was having an afternoon nap. The tubes inserted into his nose made him look sinister, like some creature that had been created in a lab. He couldn't hurt anyone now, or at least not physically anyway.

"You know everything?" Wren asked.

Jordan nodded. "Sheriff Fisher told me."

They continued to stare at the comatose Cedric for a while longer. Every time a piece of machinery made a noise her stomach lurched, wondering whether this was it, was he waking up?

"You need to know that man is not your father," said Wren. "Garrett was your father."

"It doesn't change the fact that Cedric killed my parents and left me with a gene that might mean I get cancer one day." He closed the curtain on Cedric. "I'm going to get myself some tests done. I've had a bad stomach lately, as you remember from all the wind I've been passing. I need to know if there's something wrong."

She nodded as he clutched her hand.

"I wish I'd known Dad was gay," Jordan admitted. "I wish I'd known how it was eating him inside."

"It doesn't bother you that he was cheating on your mom?" Wren asked.

"It does, but he was a good man, and I know how guilty it would've been making him." He sighed. "I don't know what to think. My mom lied to me her whole life. My dad lied to me and to himself. They were deeply flawed people, but I loved them."

Wren spotted Anthony talking to her mother at the end of the corridor. He looked upset. Dot kissed him on the cheek and walked away.

She's just broken up with him. Poor Mom.

"Anyway," said Jordan. "I'm selling the Metropolis and heading back to college tomorrow. I'm never coming back to Snowflake Bay ever again."

Wren nodded. "I understand."

He squeezed her hands. "I didn't use you for sex because I was horny or bored or because I wanted to see what it was like with an older woman. I really did want you. You made me feel special, and we had some good times, but... it wasn't love."

"It wasn't love for me either."

"I'll always remember you."

He kissed her on the lips, lingering for what felt like forever. When they parted she smiled and watched him leave.

A FEW DAYS LATER WREN was sitting on her front porch with Fiona, drinking iced coffee. She'd made it herself and it was quite delicious. The weather wasn't up to much, but the orange fall leaves that littered the street more than made up for it.

"How is the shoulder?" Fiona asked.

"Better now that you've given it a little bit of angel healing," said Wren. "But I think it'll scar. Every time I see it, I'll be reminded of that awful man."

"Just don't think about it."

A car pulled up. Wren jumped out of her seat when she saw her father and mother getting out. They looked a little ruffled, and she suspected the worst.

"You sure took your time!" she shouted, stopping in front of her dad. He wasn't giving anything away. "Your court hearing finished an hour ago."

"Your mother and I headed home to celebrate," said Wick. He winked at Dot. "We've just... finished."

Wren grimaced, but persevered. "You're not locked up, so I assume it was not guilty?"

Her mother looked away, trying to stop herself from crying.

"No, not exactly," said Wick. "Reba did brilliantly. She told the judge all about you being shot, and the death threats, and my gambling addiction, and we agreed that I serve six months in prison with a further ten years' probation, and I have to go to gambler's anonymous. It's not what I wanted, but it's better than I deserve"

Wren didn't know what to say.

"That's not good," said Wren, finally. "I don't want you to go to jail."

"I deserve it," Wick stated. "I robbed people in my town."

"When do you have to hand yourself in?" Fiona asked.

"Tomorrow morning," Wick answered. "Until then I want to spend time with my family."

Wren hugged her father, determined not to cry. This was the best outcome they could have gotten. If this has gone to a trial with a jury, he could've gotten years.

How am I going to say goodbye?

THE PARTY HAD BEEN going full swing for hours now. They'd drank and sung karaoke and told stories. It had been marvelous, just the four of them. Her father had even remarked at one point that Fiona felt like she was part of the family. If only he knew.

After a while Wren needed fresh air. She found herself on the front porch again, staring up at the stars. The cats were sat on the front lawn, all in a row. They were up to something, but she wasn't sure what. It was best to leave them to it.

Are they waiting for something?

A van pulled up outside the house across the street. It was then that Wren noticed that the for-sale sign was gone. Had someone bought the house? Why were they moving in during the middle of the night?

A man got out of the car. He was wearing a very familiar coat. He looked across the road and waved at her. When his eyes caught on the three cats he put his hands to his mouth in shock.

"Rocky?" he called. It was Benedict. "Is that you?"

He ran across the road, and Gracie's new ginger friend leapt up into his arms, rubbing against his cheek. The man was almost in tears.

"This cat is yours?" Wren asked, walking up to him. "What a small world."

"Rocky's been missing for ten days," said Benedict. He was on the verge of tears. "I've missed him so much."

"He's been hanging around my cats," Wren explained. "I thought he was a stray."

"It's weird he ended up here," said Benedict. "How did he know I'd bought this house?"

"Cats are mysterious creatures."

He smiled and put his precious feline back on the grass. The cat ran to join his friends and they disappeared around the side of the house to play.

She laughed as Benedict's familiarity seemed obvious now. "That night on the pier. I've been through so much since then. It feels like a lifetime ago. Why did you have a British accent?"

He looked guilty. "I was thinking about retiring Bieber McIntyre and becoming some sort of Helen Mirren type. I was using the accent everywhere. It was driving my friends mad." He looked solemn for a moment. "I read about you in the local papers. I heard you got shot in the leg by a deranged serial killer. That's nasty."

"I got shot in the arm, and Cedric wasn't a serial killer. He only killed two people. I think you have to kill three people to be a serial killer?" She couldn't believe she knew that. It made her sound macabre. "I'd like to say I've been through worse but I'd lying. But I'm fine. Perfectly fine."

"It's okay not to be fine."

"I am fine. Really."

Before she knew what was happening Benedict was pulling her into a hug. She leaned into his strong chest and cried, letting out all her grief and frustrations of the last week. It felt good.

Wren pulled away and wiped at her eyes. "Thanks for that. I needed a good cry."

"I'm always here," he offered.

She smiled. "Thanks."

He gave her a wink and walked back across the street, Rocky the cat in his arms. Wren headed back inside to re-join the party.

177

About the Author

C. Farren is better known as paranormal fantasy author Cate Farren. She loves cats, coffee, and watching Drag Race.

www.ingramcontent.com/pod-product-compliance
Lightning Source LLC
Chambersburg PA
CBHW021359150726
47989CB00005B/2311